MW00331815

Limo Bill

the Undercover

Assassin

By

Bill Ames

OPENING STATEMENT

To begin with, you need to realize this is a novel. All stories told are fiction. Any resemblance to any real people, places and things that have happened to, happened at or happened because of are coincidental. All characters are fictitious. Certain Landmarks in Myrtle Beach have been used to give the reader a perspective if the reader has been in Myrtle Beach and other locations in the stories. The author has received no compensation from any businesses or other landmarks in this book. In no way did anything happen exactly according to how the story is told. Again this is fictional.

That being said, the main character is based on the real Limo Bill's driving experiences in Myrtle Beach and wishes he could be the character for a day. Some experiences are partly real and most with imagination. All character references and names are not real but fictionally used to enhance the creative storytelling. Furthermore, there is no real assassin and the sexuality is purely fictional with no basis on any real experience. The random limo stories are seeded from some real stories but altered to keep it fictional. Any similarities are coincidental.

Wow, now you can let your imagination lose and get lost in the many characters used in this book. It has some fascinating imagination from start to finish. In reality, it would be hard to see most of this actually happen in real life but it sure makes for great reading. Life in Myrtle Beach is not as insane as it might appear in this book. That's why it's called fiction.

After all, what happens in Myrtle Beach – Stays in Myrtle Beach or does it?

INTRODUCTION TO AN INSANE STORY

The main character lets you get in his head narrating the many story lines. The main character, Limo Bill, is a paid assassin who only kills bad people. His cover is a Limo driver in Myrtle Beach. His partner, Annie, has a cover job as a stripper.

There are:

- Limo stories
- Assassin stories
- Party stories
- Sex stories
- Romance

Enjoy the ride in the imagination of Limo Bill.

Chapter 1

"What the hell, where the f@&$ is my panties" a loud yell came from the back of the limo. I replied sarcastically, "Don't look at me," and started to laugh with a grin on my face knowing one of the dudes in the back had a new Myrtle Beach memento.

She grilled all 3 and never got the answer, the truth from any of them. Just a ton of laughter and fingers pointing all around but her panties mysteriously disappeared. Ya, right! Even she thought it was hilarious and quickly pulled up her sexy short bright pink skirt.

We arrived to party central at Broadway at the Beach, a Louisiana style courtyard of clubs known as Celebrations. They were intoxicated but upright as they stepped out of the limo's doors. I waited there with a wry smile on my face, door open, and reached out to take her hand and help her out.

"You promise you will be here to take us back at 2" Natalia asked. "Of course darling, you know I would never leave you stranded, the dudes, well that's up to you." She was a local client of mine and although quite wild some tequila nights, she was a diversion from the simple, boring clients I sometimes pick up. These three, like other guys in the past, I had not met before.

She attracts the wild partiers and every night with her is an adventure. Sometimes I end up being her bodyguard if they try to take advantage of my sweet Natalia. She called me the next day to ask if I took her home. Just to mess with her, I'd say no but I found your panties. I could feel her blushing on the phone.

It was a good night, a fun group and a nice tip, if they only knew how wasted they looked at the end of the night.

Now that the weekend is over for my cover job, I get to relax and prepare my files for upcoming engagements. Oh ya, I forgot to mention the fact that I am an assassin. I only kill bad people though. Really, when I am commissioned a new hit, I only hear about the bad stuff. That is the justification I use to proceed and complete the job.

My assistant Annie is incredibly hot. Tall, blond with legs that never seem to end, she resembles Marilynn Monroe at first, second and third glance. When guys start wearing those beer goggles, she starts seeing green. Yep, she is the most requested stripper in Myrtle Beach and the money just flows her way. She moves in ways the body wasn't meant to.

Focus Bill. She is my gal who handles my files, yes paper files, and keeps me on point to complete each job. When they say "Behind every good man is a good woman," I hardly think this is what they had in mind. She is the best and makes my life easier.

So how does this all work? We have one handler; he's nicknamed The Grinch. I mean, he's about as ugly as the Grinch, never smiles and squints when you talk to him so I've heard. I have never met him. This fact has kept our relationship incognito.

The Grinch receives a request for end of life and once the financials are arranged, I receive a dossier with the target and contact information. From there I have 2 choices. First, go to them and complete the deed or second, lure them to Myrtle Beach and make it happen.

I prefer the second method since I have a large number of acquaintances at my disposal to help get them here. They have no clue what's about to happen to them and neither do my many contacts. Only Annie and The Grinch know the method I use.

Today is a new day on the beach. The ocean is calm with small waves; the summer crowd is beginning to stake their territory on the warming sand with towels, chairs, coolers and umbrellas. I can see guys with sun burned beer bellies and ladies in fashionable one piece and bikini bathing suits everywhere and a small group playing Frisbee along the edge of the water. From my beach house, you can look out to the ocean and it never ends. A few puffy clouds disrupt the blue skies but still picture perfect.

My phone gets a text and the code is displayed. Well, it's time. A job is being sent to my secure laptop with a specially designed code. It had been 10 days since my last job. I have to get in the right mental state before I get started. A quick call to Annie tells me payment is set up upon completion. It was a big job worth $1.3 million to my employer.

The mark is Randall Gomes, an aggressive drug distributor in Miami who has spread his territory into the wrong direction, our client's turf. I don't care why, but it's interesting to hear the why. Some of our client's men met their demise and he isn't going to allow Gomes to get away with it.

Time to get to work. First, I need to lay out my plan. Miami isn't far but I would prefer to lure him away from his home turf. I don't particularly care to deal with drug dealers as a job but the money is always good because of the risk and reward for a successful hit.

I called on my friendly bartender Jose, who is from Miami. He gave me a better understanding of Gomes' area and the drug trade there. He appreciated the three bills I laid on him for the information. Jose is one of my many contacts in Myrtle I can rely on for information.

It seems unlikely I can lure him to Myrtle Beach with all that is happening in Miami. Gomes has a place he likes to take his ladies for a special night. He has a penthouse at the Franklin Ritz Hotel in South Beach. So that's the target to plan for.

The knock on the door was a sweet sound to my ears. The most intoxicating woman I know stood there inches from me and all I could do was give her a kiss on the cheek and invite her in. Annie came by to help me brainstorm for the best method of reaching him, business first.

We decided to have her join us along with her redheaded friend Molly. No matter where they go, they draw attention and that is what we count on. Plane leaves in 8 hours, our plans are set so it's time to play.

This time, when Annie got within inches, I pulled her toward me and kissed her on the lips like it's supposed to happen when lovers get together.

This woman is a knockout. She could be with anyone and I had her attention. Life is great I thought. We had some us time and took full advantage of it. After following each other's lead and removing our clothes I gently laid her on the bed. Foreplay was short and sweet and we shared our horny lust.

Being a stripper, I always wonder if her orgasm is real or is she faking it. I'm going with for real. Hey, I'm a guy. That's how it's supposed to be. We switched positions with her on top. I could tell she was weakened but was quickly back in rare form. She slid her body across mine and sent me into another world. I felt every inch of her body and when she offered herself again, I excitedly made the most of the opportunity.

We thrust against each other for some time before it was my turn to reach the ultimate moment of pleasure. I didn't want it to stop but nature took its course. We laid in each other's arms. I leaned over and gave her another sensual kiss. As we parted, she smiled at me. Time for some sleep, we leave in 7 hours to lift off.

Chapter 2

As we gathered our suitcases to leave for the airport, we discussed the plan one more time. One mistake and we could be eliminated from our playful lives. The limo was here for us and we proceeded to the airport. After getting through security without a delay, we waited at the Southwest terminal.

I noticed one of my clients was catching a flight also. Carl was in town to play some golf even though it was too hot for most. Heat didn't bother his play, but for me, heat wears me out by the 9th hole. He didn't care as much about the golf as he did his riding companion from the Myrtle Beach Caddie Girls. He always called on the lovely Cameron with the huge smile and shapely body to caddie for him. I think if he broke 100, it was a win-win kind of day.

He came over and shook my hand and immediately moved his attention to Annie. He said she looked familiar but couldn't place it but kept staring at her and then it clicked. A few nights ago, at the GFE Gentlemen's Club, he missed out on a dance with her to his buddy Sam. He never saw Sam or Annie again that night after they departed to the Champagne room.

It's time to board the plane so we shook hands again and started to go our separate ways. He looked back and said, "I'll call you when I'm back in town in September." I smiled and said "You bet."

———————————

The flight was uneventful and that's a good thing. Before we knew it, the plane was on the approach to Miami International. After collecting our luggage, Annie and I grabbed a taxi to The Franklin Ritz Hotel and checked in.

We already had confirmed Gomes was staying in the penthouse suit for 2 days. There were signs of security beefed up inside and outside of the Ritz. Today was purely an observation day and for Annie and Molly who met us there to get noticed by members of Gomes's security. I need their help to get close to Gomes within 24 hours.

After loading our luggage into our room, we headed to the lobby for quick refreshment. It's only noon so there is plenty of time to make an impression. I ordered a Vodka and Coke, Annie and Molly had some type of blue beachy drink with an umbrella and a sliced orange for decoration. It didn't take long and all the eyes were on the ladies. I must have been invisible but that's cool.

As Annie and Molly chatted up with subtle laughter and the occasional glance to the men in the lobby, I could tell our plan was working. They were touchy feely with each other and that was getting even more attention than their incredible looks. It was time to move to the pool area.

Being seen as tourists was important. We needed to fit in to the visual perception as playful partiers. After about 30 minutes, I bought drinks for everyone at the Tiki bar. I now had dozens of new friends to mingle with. I told them I recently I came into some family money and I wanted to shake things up. They all wanted a part of that.

As we reached evening, our loud party had grown to nearly 40 people and it got the attention of Gomes. He came to join us with his trio of smoking hot women and with six giant beefy steroid type bodyguards.

Several of the women tried to get with them but they resisted like true professionals. I'm sure that if they did partake in the ladies interest, they would be shot on sight or at least behind closed doors.

This was going better than I had planned. One of the bodyguards presented a note to me and asked me if we'd like to join him at Baoli. He is a major VIP there with an open invitation. Bring the girls if you want to come. I knew where this was going. He wanted Annie and Molly for his pleasure.

It was important to keep our cover and get close to him to complete our task. We agreed and made plans to refresh and meet at 11 p.m. in the lobby. I needed to get the next part of the plan in place.

Back in the room, Annie and Molly changed from beach attire to party dresses with low cut tops and extremely short skirts. Annie's dress was a glistening silver color and Molly's was gold. No bra and a thong if you could call it that. They were legendary to look at.

I had my traditional party outfit. Black slacks, shoe boots, black short sleeve shirt and my blazer with the EOL (end of life drug). What's that you ask? I have a great doctor. Dr. Randi. Dr. Randi is my scientist acquaintance who makes my special potion for death. I forgot to mention earlier she is the one other person who knows what I do.

She has developed an elixir that when injected into the bloodstream, will create a blood clot that will travel to the heart and an immediate heart attack occurs with no chance of survival. The special part is the delivery system is designed to wait 24 hours before activating.

This gives me plenty of time to depart, have an alibi if needed and avoid any chance of being connected to the targets demise. You've got to love science. I pay her quite well to keep me exclusively supplied. What's even better is EOL is encased in the form of a band aid with a small needle to inject the subject. The band aide turns green confirming EOL was dispensed.

The entry is so undetectable and has no prickly feel to it so no one ever knows they've been injected unless I was to tell them. The drug takes nanoseconds to dispense and is designed to expand once in the bloodstream.

Now you know the how, let's get to the event.

ʌ

Chapter 3

We all meet in the lobby and the limo is waiting outside taking us to the club. It was just Gomes, Annie, Molly, his three ladies and I. We introduced ourselves to Gomes; my name was Peter Evans, the name I checked in as. The girls were Amanda and Sally. Whenever Molly joined us, we told her we were role playing with fake names. This would help us avoid repercussions if things went bad. This was fun for her just like role playing in the bedroom and as a stripper.

We were soon at Baoli and never having been there before, I was impressed. However, all I could think of was the task at hand. With all these thugs around, timing has to be precise to get out of here alive.

The liquor, wine and champagne flowed freely. The music was so inviting and easy to simply live in the moment and get caught up in the club atmosphere. Focus Bill, pick your moment. Annie and Molly were in their element, tons of men paying full attention to them.

Annie walked over to Gomes and started to grind a lap dance and despite several men ready to remove her, Gomes raised his hand indicating its OK. Molly then followed and wrapped her arms caressingly about his shoulders and neck. He looked at me, grinned and sent his girls to do the same with me. I didn't expect it, but it was a fine gesture on his part.

Hours passed and we engaged in a surprisingly interesting conversation about life in Miami. The subject of his business was real estate, how much he owned and how much he planned on owning. I explained my money was inherited from parents who had real estate fortunes in New York and Boston. It was easy to converse about something he could never check up on. I looked at him, "I won't ask if you don't ask." That ended this discussion.

He loved X (Known as The Horny Pill which is a natural version of Viagra with a loving effect like ecstasy but without the bad effects) and had all the girls in the group partake along with he and I.

It was a challenge but I used slight of hands to avoid taking it when Annie realized I needed a diversion and pulled up her skirt and every eye was on her and not me as I pretended to swallow the X. "Great work," I whispered to her and she broke out into a loud hilarious laugh as though I told the best joke in the world.

When the effects began taking hold, the smiles were cute, funny and amazing depending on who you were looking at. My eyes were focused on Gomes and I knew it was time so I secured the EOL in the palm of my hands. The ladies started dancing moments ahead of us so we joined in. As we traded partners and he started groping my gals, I wanted to give him a double dose but one would do.

The music stopped momentarily and Gomes was handed a microphone. Placing it to his lips while looking out at the crowd, he blurts "I love Miami!" and the crowd went wild. Many knew who he really was and acted like they were honored to be in his presence. Idiots I thought to myself. It's about to change for him.

He yelled "I love you all," like a little kid. The X had done its job. I grabbed the microphone and started laughing to play up the X and yelled, "Isn't he the greatest!" That sent the crowd into a cheer as I put my hand firmly on his neck injecting him with EOL. I smiled and said "Thanks for the incredible night my friend. If you're up for a lunch tomorrow, let's meet at the hotel restaurant." He said, "Sounds good."

Annie and Molly were all lit up and very friendly. About an hour later, nearly 3 a.m., we left Gomes and his entourage to continue partying. All I knew is the deed is done and I just want to get away from here as soon as possible without raising red flags.

Chapter 4

I had a call from an old friend. He said he just broke up with his girl and needed a night out. Maybe a trip to Broadway at the Beach would do the trick. We set a time for 9 p.m. and I promised I would be there.

9 o'clock was fast approaching and I was near the hotel he was staying at. Pulling around the front office, I could see him in the distance. It appeared he was having an argument with his girl who I thought he broke up with.

He walked up to me and we shook hands only to be harassed by the young lady yelling in his ear. He told her it was over but she wanted nothing to do with those words. "Please don't act like this to me," she said to him. "Listen girl, we are done. Get your ass away from me." She still insisted on being with him and he went into the Limo through the door I had opened.

Before I could close the door, she jumped alongside him. I wasn't really sure what to do at this point. It's his problem or I should it's their problem so I jumped in the driver's seat and put it in drive. I could see hands flying on her part and he was yelling back at her.

Not a comfortable position for me to be in. I drove very slowly down Ocean Boulevard at maybe 15 miles per hour waiting for any indication she might be getting out or making the trip. He kept repeating they were done because she cheated on him and she's simply a royal bitch.

I'm sure the issue is on both sides knowing him. Whatever their issues, I just wanted it to settle down. I turned back and asked if everything was OK even though it clearly wasn't. He said to keep on going.

The next thing I hear is a door opening while I'm driving and before I could react, I see her in my side view mirror rolling down Ocean Boulevard. I slammed on my breaks and rushed out the door to help her and she simply got up and ran away.

He never moved an inch. It was all her with the insane exit. I stepped back into the Limo and turned to him saying, "It's a good thing I was only going 15 when she jumped."

He didn't hesitate a second saying, "You should have been going 50," and started to laugh.

No love lost there!

Chapter 5

The weekend starts tomorrow and I have a bachelorette group who has booked me for the night. I found out the bachelor party was in my limo a few weeks ago. Early 20's, a best man who was a player and a groom who I could tell really loved his fiancé but still had a wild side. They started out with dinner at Yamato's Japanese Steakhouse and some clubbing at Sr. Frogs and then wherever the ladies were.

Finally at midnight, they hit the strip club circuit Myrtle Beach offers. I didn't go inside with them. Plausible deniability is my story. I did get a hold of Annie to make his night memorable. She told me he was too willing at first and then backed out for fear of his fiancé. Good move on his part. That sure took some will power to turn down Annie.

This time it was the girl's night out. A group of 9 stunners in high heels were all single except for the two of them who were married. The party group was now on their way down. They were in their early 20's and you could tell a few of them didn't get out much. Parked out front of the Breakers Resort, they begin to enter the Limo with tall drinks in hand including penis straws and the bride to be, Katy, had penis' pinned all over her top.

The valet and security guys were loving it after seeing them partying by the pool all day. 9 girls with short black dresses, sashes that say bridesmaid all in stiletto heels and a bride who cannot hide the fact approached the Limo. They were like a billboard for trouble with all the guys who gravitate to this exact scenario. Somebody was getting laid tonight.

It was a Kodak moment sure to land on my website, facebook, twitter, pinterest, tumbler and instagram. Not by me, (ha ha) but before the end of the night with all their cameras popping flashes like paparazzi in the back of the Limo. It's easy PR for me. I keep them safe and let them have fun. Sometimes it's too much. It just depends on how many bad girls are in the mix.

Putting 9 skinny girls in my limo who have been drinking for hours without dinner, disaster awaits. I doubt most will make it to 2 am. As we arrive, more pictures are taken, all heads from the crowd entering Broadway swiveled to them and guys are whistling already.

I gave them instructions where I will be in case anyone needs to go back to the resort. It is 10 p.m. and party time is in the very early stages of the night. Families were still finishing dinner and shopping in Broadway at the Beach.

There's a large family of seven with balloons on their heads and dog shaped balloons, heart shapes, a house and many more designs. Those balloon makers in Sr. Frogs are good and make a killing with their expertise.

By 11 o'clock, the clubs are hopping and the crowd piles in. By midnight, it's not uncommon to see lines out the door on the weekends because of the fire limits for people in the building. Tonight was no exception.

About 1 am, I get the first call. "Hello, hello, hello," is all I could barely make out from the noise in the background. Then they hang up. At that point, I sent a text to them telling them to step outside and call me or text me back. About 20 minutes later another call. "Hewo, hewo it's Katy!"

"Hey Katy, are you ready yet?" "Maybe in 20 um 20 um mintz, I go to find everyone." She is definitely toasted. "OK, just let me know, I'm here if anyone is ready to come out." "Kkkkkkkkkk, you're the best, I Wuv you Wimo Bill." If I had a dollar........ Bleep beep, she hung up.

The good news is the night is nearly over, the not so good news, I have no idea the condition they're in. Every time I think I've seen it all, somebody derails that theory. Fortunately it's a short ride back and the risk of someone heaving is less likely but still real.

My phone is ringing again, "Hey iz Kadddddddy. We're cominnnn outttt." Bleep beep. Oh boy, the anticipation at this point is worth the wait. Here they come. They are one of four groups in black dresses tonight but by far the cutest. After all, they are my clients.

Katy has her shoes in her hand. I could tell she fell at least once with the floor dust used for dance floors all over her behind. "There's my favorite person in the whole world, I wuv youuuuu Wimo Bill, thanks for cominnn (burp) cominnnn to get us."

We shared a hug and I lead her into the Limo. One after another, they pile in. A few had me worried. I pointed them out to the rest and reminded them if anyone spewed, it's a $200 cleanup fee. Only those close to sober understood.

I did a head count and only counted 8. "Who are we missing, I only count 8 and we started with 9." They all looked around, "Sara, anyone see Sara?" Out of the corner of my eye I see a hand in the front seat raise. "Here" Somehow she slipped into the front seat to ride shotgun. I closed the door and put it in drive. "Stop! Stop! stop!"

I slammed the breaks and bodies start rolling forward. The back door opens and Katy let loose while her friends held her hair. That was a close moment and yet another Kodak moment. It all landed outside. I gave her some napkins and a bottle of water and away we went.

7 minutes later we arrived at the Breakers and out they came. I was wrong about someone getting laid tonight. Not a single lady was in condition to continue the night. There will be some stories to tell and hangovers to deal with in the morning. The future of this wedding looks as safe as ever. Kevin my man, (the groom to be) I wish you good luck buddy.

Chapter 6

When I woke up in the afternoon, I checked out the new headlines on my computer. Next to the top of the list was the surprising story that Gomes had died of a heart attack at the same nightclub around 2:30 a.m.

Apparently he had some health conditions and had an appointment with his doctors the following week. Exactly according to plan, the heart attack theory was an easy explanation and it is one more job that can't be traced back to me or Annie.

Later that night, Annie joined me for dinner at Ciao to celebrate with a bottle of wine and a romantic celebratory exquisite Italian meal. She had the night off like I did so we took in a movie at Market Commons and she stayed the night with me on the beach.

In the morning, the transfer for $1,000,000 was completed to our bank in an undisclosed location. That's right, that's for us to know and you're not to ever find out. Annie is my assistant but really my partner. Half of everything in the account is hers after expenses of course.

It's a very unique relationship. In a world of who can you really trust, we trust each other explicitly. What we have works despite the many facets of our crazy lives. At the end of the day, we have each other's back in business and as lovers.

The next job is scheduled for the Friday of next week. Johnny Jacobs of Boston is the new mark. He ran over our clients 2 kids while under the influence of crack cocaine. According to the Grinch, the client wants justice and closure for his family if that is ever possible. The job is for the minimum $1 mil and after the Grinch's cut, $800,000 will be our cut upon completion.

Johnny boy will be an easier mark than our last. For starters, he loves golf, night clubs, the beach and the ladies. Myrtle Beach has it all. We have a plethora of Bostonians here in Myrtle. I asked a few of those I know locally for a special I could offer a good client for next Friday. Tray from Westgate and Aaron from the Caribbean resort had penthouse suites available.

From the files, we noticed he worked in the John F. Kennedy Federal Building. Somehow he was able to get out on bail until his trial which was in 3 weeks. His employer for some reason let him keep working using the innocent until proven guilty theory.

This was a nearly a slam dunk case yet his very expensive lawyer got him out with a tracer on his ankle and every other day drug testing. Needless to say, there are some complications we didn't count on, particularly with the ankle bracelet.

In his dossier, a nice surprise was inside. He had a very rich uncle he never met who lived in Europe. If we played it right, we could convince him that he heard about his plight and wanted to help this one time.

The Plan A thought was for him to receive a promotional contest winning certificate to Myrtle Beach with Limo service from the airport to night clubs and a penthouse weekend stay.

Annie and I started brainstorming about different scenarios to complete this without being detected anywhere in the deal, getting him next to us and sending him on the way during the 24 timer EOL has. Getting creative is what makes this business fun, and of course, the money. Never forget the money and one less bad guy in the world.

She had to work that night so we planned on discussing our options the next day. I never visit her at work unless I have a Limo client or a job to do. It's how it keeps from feeling weird. It won't be long and our cover jobs aren't needed and we can try and live a normal life.

Chapter 7

Annie is home and I'm on my way. It's great having a place on the beach. Overlooking the ocean and the beach full of vacationers all summer and then the silence of the offseason, it's priceless. Having my beautiful partner prancing around practically naked most days is the other awesome view I'm forced to live with.

As I walk in, I'm startled by a hard bodied guy sitting at the kitchen table sipping on a glass of red wine. This is not normal and I wanted an explanation. Immediately he said, "I'm Drake" as he extended his hand toward me for a handshake.

"Hi, I'm Bill and you're in my house why?" "I met Annie at the club last night and I understand you were following the trial for Johnny Jacobs of Boston. It's a real tragedy. Two young children run over. He ought to be crucified."

"Ya, I hate the news and all the negativity I see on TV. So, how do you Drake?" I asked. "I played golf with him a couple of years ago here in Myrtle and thought he was reckless then. Annie said a friend of yours was trying to contact the family and offer your condolences."

"That's right, my friend new the Nolan's from years ago as neighbors." "I could get the info for you if you want?" "Sure, that would be great." I said.

"Here comes Annie," I said as she comes walking up the steps leading from the beach. "Hi honey, I bumped into Drake on the beach and after the impression he made last night, (Drake showered her with 2K in the champagne room) I thought the least I could do is offer him a drink. What a coincidence about the Jacobs connection?" " For sure, it really is."

"Hey, thanks for the wine. I have to meet my family at Nascar Park. If I find their info, I'll drop it by. You have a great place." "Thanks, well, you better get back to your family." Drake leaves and I just look at Annie. She's like "What? I was just following up about the Jacobs case. Besides, he's married."

"Ya, but you know how I feel about bringing men into my house." "I know, jealous?" "Damn right!" I felt like a teenager all over again, especially since he was so hot looking like a calendar boy or movie star. How dare she. Then I thought, at the end of the day she is with me. There, all better Bill.

Hours later we discussed the Jacobs case. We have serious concerns about bringing him here and trying to stay anonymous through the process. All the questions we've been asking could add to red flags if he dies in Myrtle. It's still plan A but we have a lot to work out. Plan B is to take care of business in Boston and get back to Myrtle quickly.

Plan B includes learning who his drug supplier is and make a special delivery to Jacobs on his way from work. It means moving the operation to Boston and learning his route, habits and other nuances. I'm beginning to like plan B better. I'll sleep on it. I have another bachelorette group tomorrow night to attend to.

Annie was being a big tease today. She got the rise out of me when I walked in and saw Drake at the table. Annie has a lot of girlfriends. No surprise considering the exotic dancer business to be politically correct. She invited Bridgette over for drinks and some company. Little did I know it was for her? Annie was being bad, really tapping that jealous gene of mine.

The doorbell rang and I answered the door and of course, it was Bridgette, all 6 foot of her with jet black hair down to her ass. When she stood sideways, her figure was straight out of Playboy. Annie told her casual so she wore her bikini with a see through white mesh sun dress.

Let's move down to the hot tub on the deck and bring our wine. A beautiful evening with a full moon glistening off the ocean is a heavenly sight for everyone. And that's why I live on the beach.

The messaging effects of the jets were hypnotic. I felt more relaxed than sexually stimulated with two gorgeous women in the same hot tub. Soon, we had finished a couple of bottles of wine. "Babe, could you get us some more wine?" "Sure thing sweetie" I retreated back into the house for 2 more bottles. As I popped the corks, I looked out the kitchen window overlooking the hot tub and all I saw was two bodies as one.

They were in a deep embrace, kissing slowly and moving up and down each other's neck with passion. Now I was ready for my time with Annie. But, I couldn't deny their moment and just enjoyed the scenery.

After 20 more minutes, I couldn't wait any longer. I brought a bottle in each hand to rejoin the ladies. They ignored me and kept their spirited moment going. So I drank more wine and began to move in.

As I started to press my body against Annie, she reached back and pushed me away and giggled. I thought, hey wait a minute.

She knew she was driving me wild. I moved toward her again and this time she and Bridgette got out of the tub, grabbed a bottle of wine and headed to our bedroom.

"Bitch!" They both broke into laughter. "Bitches!" I was humiliated and more jealous than ever. As I was planning my next move, they both came out of the bedroom laughing hysterically. All I could do is hold my arms out like what the hell are you up to. A knock on the door answered my question.

It was my good buddy Allan. He was there for Bridgette. Annie had set them up and he was here to take her to a private party for some of his friends. We were invited also. It was a plan. Bridgette and Allan left and we had about an hour to get ready and be at the party.

"You've been a bad girl Annie" "Whatever do you mean?" she said sarcastically. "You played off the jealousy from Drake and Bridgette and now you're going to get it." "I sure hope so Limo Bill." "Wise ass," I said under my breath but loud enough for her to hear me. "To the bedroom now," returning the sarcasm.

"Time for a new toy my dear but first the blindfold." She closed her eyes and accepted my demands. I placed the blindfold on, reached down and fondled her breasts, kissed her on the lips and all I could smell was the perfume Bridgette was wearing. It was like cheating without cheating.

I opened the box containing the new toy, I waited for the right moment to implement and after today, this was it. Remote controlled vibrator with a thong harness to keep it in place. I tied her hands to the bed posts to keep her from stopping me although I seriously doubt she would.

"What are you up to tonight?" "You'll see my lady, you'll see or should I say I'll see and you'll feel it all night." Her mind swirled with a bunch of scenarios but there wasn't anything she could do about it.

After I sexed her up a little, I took the device and placed it between her legs and she shrieked. As I added the harness and locked it in place, she had an idea it was a thin chastity device but didn't know it was a remote controlled device with a vibrator inside.

It was now time to get ready to leave so I untied her, removed the blindfold and said don't touch. "Your wish is my command," she said, still unsure of what I was up to. She slipped on one of her miniskirts and away we went.

When we arrived at Allan's house, also on the beach, you could hear the party was underway. Bridgette opened the door and ushered us in to grab a drink. It was cool, streamers everywhere, tiki torches, plenty of alcohol, a pool and hot tub out back. Not bad for an unexpected night out.

Annie had met up with Bridgette in the other room. I pulled out the remote and started with a slow vibrating motion. Annie jumped and screamed in surprise. Only a few saw her reaction and asked if she was OK. "Yep, I'm fine" she replied with a blushing look on her face.

Then I got the stare. I held up the remote and raised the level. I could see she now knew what it was and started to blush and twitch. Paybacks a bitch I thought after the earlier events of the day.

Actually I got the idea from the movie "The Ugly Truth" which offered one of the most hilarious dinner meetings I've ever seen. Throughout the night I would raise and lower the vibration level. I totally had her attention now.

It was an interesting ride home. She was totally turned on and so was I. She practically started ripping off my clothes before we got into the door. She was completely naked in the car except for the vibrator. We opened the door and hustled straight to the bedroom but I wasn't done yet. I still had control of the remote control and I raised it a few notches to increase the buzz Annie was feeling. I could see her blushing and cussing me at the same time.

It was an unusual method of foreplay that worked in my favor. Annie finally gave in and moved toward me for an embrace. She somehow held it together when looking into my eyes all along knowing she was as excited as I was. I moved forward and placed my lips on hers and let our emotions take over.

I removed the remote control vibrator and then joined her on the bed for a sensational round of lovemaking. It was an incredible night brought on by all the jealousy from all the earlier events. I look forward to the next time she teases the hell out of me.

Chapter 8

Missy called me about noon to verify tonight's bachelorette schedule. 8 p.m. to 1 a.m. minimum. Dinner first at Dick's Last Resort, a 1 hour ride with their fruity drinks, some tequila and vodka red bulls and then to Broadway and club Boca and Malibu's for some wild club atmosphere.

It was a plan well thought out and for some time now. Missy is the maid of honor and is a control freak until she's drunk so I'm told by the bride to be Meagan.

The wedding is scheduled for 3 months from now leaving plenty of time for more parties. I'll wait and see them before I can assess the night and how it will probably play out.

I drive up to their place in Surfside. It's a huge beach house on stilts that can accommodate up to a dozen people with beds and pull out sofas. My group wasn't quite that large, just 8 young southern belles ready to let loose for a night. One by one they made their way down the steps.

They all had short black shorts and revealing tops with black high heeled shoes. Every single one was blond, most were natural blond. I gathered them for a picture for the website, with all their chatter, the ladies southern twang filled the airways. I thought I might go into diabetic shock they sounded so sweet.

Missy and Meagan came right over to me after taking pictures on their phones and both hugged me simultaneously. They thanked me for picking them up. A few others did the same. This is going to be an interesting night with hot young ladies who are huggers and very sweet.

It's a 40 minute drive to Dick's so we cranked the music they had on their iphones and the drinks started to pour. One young lady had a preference for the tequila. They sang to the lyrics of the songs as if it were a karaoke contest on the gong show contest. Only there hotness would keep them from getting gonged.

When we reached Dick's, I gave them a few minutes to finish their opened drinks. If you have never been to a Dick's Last Resort, their forte is to insult the guest and the guests can reply appropriately. If you are not expecting it or can't take criticism, this is not for you. I've seen many ladies with mascara running down their face, in tears and totally upset. Everyone gets this huge tall white hat and the staff writes insults on it for them.

It looks like a meeting of a Klu Klux Klan gathering when they all come out together. Some say it looks like a big white penis on their head which would be appropriate for a bachelorette group or a gay group. I've had both types of groups in my Limo and they are hilarious with their hats.

When dinner finished, the gals did good and all came out spirited and tipsier then when they went in. Those silly hats made for another set of pictures. It was now about 9:30 and the plan was Broadway and the clubs but 3 ladies started shouting, "strip club strip club strip club!" I asked which type male or female. "Male! Male! Male!" I explained a local strip club had a male review from 8 'til 1 a.m. They voted and our plans were changed.

We pulled up to the front door and most were screaming like they won the lottery. None of the girls had been to a male strip club but they all had been to a gentlemen's club. I swear it's a southern thing where many of the southern ladies vs. me being a Yankee as they call us down here, think nothing of going to a strip club. Maybe it's the younger generation.

So off they were and I just waited outside. No way was I going in there. Ten minutes later, Jenny and Michelle came out. They said, "eww," with a funny face saying they were old, bald and wrinkly. We waited about 30 minutes and the rest came out. I didn't ask

---

It was still early and Broadway at the Beach was in rare form. People were coming in bunches and the Limos, shuttles and taxis were dropping their customers off and rushing for more pickups. I waited about an hour and a half and then I went in to check on them. I figured they would be easy to spot as a group.

Sure enough, I found them in Malibu's out on the dance floor with guys they just met. I found Missy and she had some guy up against the wall swapping spit and groping each other. Yep all seemed fine.

1 a.m. was coming fast so I texted Missy about the time. She got with the rest of them to start leaving. The bride to be had a new friend and he wasn't letting go. Eventually, they all made it out with 4 guys attached. Two of the ladies were married and the bride to be didn't want to let go.

It's not my business, but nothing good was going to happen from this situation. I raised my voice saying "All the ladies in the Limo, no guys allowed on this trip. I told the girls that if they want the guys to come to jump in a taxi and follow us." A few boos was the response.

Everyone agreed to my demands and I watched the taxi follow us all the way to Surfside. I bet the guys were surprised it was a $40 cab ride and they still had to get back. My night was complete. My clients were home safe. It's the last I saw of them but I'd bet the stories they would have to tell ended up blackmail for some of them. What happens in Myrtle Beach stays in Myrtle Beach! I don't think so but people say it all the time around here.

Chapter 9

Annie stayed at her place after work. I needed my sleep anyway. I have to get back to planning the Jacobs job. Plan A or Plan B. There is so much to do for a precision effort. Every job has to be executed perfectly. This one looked easy at the start but not anymore. I've already accepted the job so there is no going back now.

I've decided to make a quick trip up to Boston on Monday and get a better look at the situation, gather some intel about the area, his route to and from work and see if the drug dealer's name can be revealed. The plan still is to complete the job by Friday. I believe I have a birthday party group next Friday in the Limo so Thursday is my official deadline.

Annie came over on Monday and we made plans to go to Boston that night and start our surveillance Tuesday morning. I'll have the EOL drug ready in case the opportunity existed.

We packed up and jumped on Spirit Airlines for a direct flight. We did carry on only since it was expected to be a short trip. We decided to get a hotel close to Jacobs' work place. We know where he's confined by his ankle bracelet.

With Annie alongside me, we hardly look like killers or someone on a stakeout. In our rental car, we drove to his apartment and look for signs of him but no luck.

He leaves at 7 a.m. in the morning to go to work. That's when we need to be here. Tonight, we'll do some clubbing and find out about the drug dealer. First, we'll grab some dinner and then get to work.

We found a featured restaurant by day and nightclub by night. This should be a good place to eat and hang.

Annie went to the ladies room and looked for the right person to ask for some crack. It didn't take long. She met a waitress who had a couple of teeth missing and simply asked her if she knew where she could score some crack in the area. She said, you buy one for me and I'll have them come here.

About 30 minutes later, a well dressed man came up to the waitress. Annie had given her $60 for 3 hits. As the gentleman left, Annie approached the waitress. Annie said if you give me a name of the biggest dealer in town, I'll let you keep all 3 hits of crack.

"Are you a cop?" "No," said Annie. I have a friend who needs a larger amount to take to Atlanta. My guy was shot and I have to find a new supplier. "Ask for Antonio the Hammer," she said quietly. "Thanks."

Now we had a name to start with, we saw Jacobs route to work and next was to set up a meeting with him on his way home. When we got back, the dossier gave us all the info on his Uncle Ted. The plan was to pretend to be Uncle Ted and explain he heard about the situation he was in and wanted to help.

He would explain he knew about the crack and if he needed that, he would arrange it for him but he needs to be anonymous and untraceable in helping him.

Later the next day, with a blocked burner phone, I made that call and everything went according to plan except the dealer wasn't Antonio who he normally gets it from. I explained it was the best I could do under the circumstances and if he wanted it, a courier would bring it to him on his way home.

He was so messed up and figuring life in prison is all he could look forward to, he ignored the red flags from the drug tests and agreed to meet the drug dealer (me) at the store 2 blocks from his job.

It was set. Boston here I come again. I made a stop in LaGuardia to avoid suspicions and rented a car. I met a contact with the crack I needed in NY and drove to Boston. I was early so I waited around the corner until his work day ended and proceeded to the parking lot we discussed. I had a wig on to change my appearance and fake tattoos with a sleeveless t-shirt to keep it looking real.

I had Jacobs sit in my car long enough to hand him cash for his defense and the package of crack. As we shook hands, I injected him with the EOL drug as I dropped the package to act as a diversion. Worked like a charm. The EOL band aid turned green, good to go. He got back in his car and off he went. It took all of about 5-7 minutes.

I put on a shirt covering up all the fake tattoos but left on the wig until I landed in Myrtle Beach. He was injected about 5 p.m. so the clock was ticking. Couldn't wait to get back to Annie and see what she was up to.

When I reached my house, I felt pretty positive about completing another job. Tomorrow the news will reveal his untimely death and we'll get paid.

Chapter 10

No time like the present, I called Annie to see what she was up to and told her I was safe at home and the job was completed. She sounded relieved and said she'll be right over.

One minute later the doorbell rings and there she is. She was already on her way when I called. I told her all about the happenings that day and I sure was glad to see her smile. We embraced and sunk into the couch and just relaxed together for a while. She said "I'm going to the hot tub, care to join me?" Well, that's a no brainer. "I'll bring the wine".

The hot tub was just what I needed. It was a stressful day and this just took all the stress away. Annie smiled at me and slid over to my side and we just held each other. Usually when a job gets done, we do it together but this was a unique situation that had to be handled quickly and I'm always the one who administers the EOL drug.

After the wine was done, we headed back inside for a quick snack, after our snack we took a shower together. She was impossible to resist. The water bouncing off here toned body, the wet hair, and that coconut scented sun tan lotion. I reached around her back and grabbed the bar of soap. Gently, I stroked in many directions until her body was engulfed in suds. She turned and did the same to me.

Grabbing the shower wand, we rinsed each other off, grabbed some towels and dried ourselves off. She was first to the bed laying there totally naked and sexy as ever. I rolled her over and laid on top of her. She felt so good.

No words were spoken, just moans filled the room and our ears as I thrust inside her and we spent the next 30 minutes enjoying foreplay and making love. This wasn't sex, this was making love. We laid there for quite a while just kissing, smiling, running our hands over each other and eventually we fell asleep in each other's arms.

It seems like lately we are in sync. I pray it never stops.

When we woke up, we made love once again. We've known each other for nearly 10 years but something has changed. Each moment together gets more special. We can be sensual, naughty, exploratory, creative and it's all good.

As the day turned to evening, we decided to have dinner at Rioz Brazilian Steakhouse. I was in the mood for some filet mignon and it's basically all you can eat. After dinner, we stopped at her place. She had one of her friends, Electra, coming to visit from Vegas. She is a fellow dancer who could pass as Annie's sister.

Just then an alert came across my phone showing our payment was complete from the Jacobs job. In reading the news blurb, it said he had a heart attack and drugs were involved. The police were looking in to who the drug dealer was as a person of interest.

Antonio the Hammer had been under surveillance by the DEA and FBI in connection with a few murders lately and he would be the cop's main focus. Also Jacobs had a stash of cash form yours truly appearing to be working a drug deal. Another perfectly executed job and no way to be traced back to us.

I headed back to my place to crash and let them do some catching up. I hear Electra is a party animal. I need some rest. This one's for Annie to handle. They had planned girl's night out with Bridgette and a few other friends from strip club.

Chapter 11

The big night arrived for Chrissy. Her 40th birthday and a limo full of friends and family with five guys and five gals ready to unleash their badness on Myrtle Beach.

They had serious money so no expense was too much. As I pulled into the Marina Grand Dunes, the valet met me with smiles and George the head valet asked, "Here for the McMichael party." "Yep, that's who I'm here for. I'm a few minutes early so no rush."

George replied, "They're in the bar, I'll go let them know you are here," as he reached his hand out for the 20 spot I slid into his hand. George was a good guy. He's been here since the resort's opening and when I met him last year, we hit it off and he sends business my way.

Tonight I was driving the Hummer. This was a high roller group that wanted the best. I had coolers ready with Champaign as requested by Jim, Chrissy's boyfriend. Six bottles of the finest bubbly I could get my hands on. Just a sample of what's to come.

"Hot Damn, we gonna get F&%$ed up tonight". Really moron I thought to myself. And who says hot damn anymore. Of course he's the loud one in the group who always has to be heard. He was wearing a camouflage shirt and a Stetson which did look cool.

Go figure, his name is Big G. Hugs from the ladies and handshakes with the guys and we were new BF's. All the lights were spinning inside, music blaring and ladies screaming like they were in a contest.

First stop was Duck's to do some shaggin' (South Carolina's state dance) and of course drinking. Main Street in North Myrtle Beach isn't the widest of streets so temporarily parking in front of Duck's caused some traffic issues. About an hour later, they were ready to go to Broadway at the Beach.

For 40 somethings, they had the party bug in them. It was like a race to consume as much as possible on this 30 minute trip. A quick glance in the mirror, they were doing lap dances. Girls on guys, girls on girls, guys on girls and dare I say it, guys on guys. No doubt they were all good friends and this wasn't their first rodeo.

Chrissy leaned in through the window separating me from the back and whispered, "It's my birthday Mr. Bill." I chuckled, "It most definitely is." "Could I tell you a secret?" "Sure" She nibbled on my ear and said, "We're swingers and I want you." I didn't see that coming. "If I wasn't working, you'd be all mine." I said jokingly.

She reached further in, practically gave me a hickey and putting her boob in my face. I swerved off the road and hit the brakes hard. If you've ever been in a limo, slamming the brakes hard sends everyone not in a seatbelt, rolling forward. Now that was a funny scene watching bodies flying all around and ending up in compromising positions. Two of the ladies basically lost their skirts when it rose up their hips.

"Is everyone OK?" as I looked at Chrissy. A voice from the floor blurted, "Do it again!" Of course it was Big G. One more light and we'd be pulling into Broadway at the Beach. We made our way to the Hard Rock Café circle, our Limo drop off spot to the club area. The ladies adjusted their skirts and hair and exited the Limo. I lead them over to Crocodile Rocks to get them in free and party to the Dueling Piano's. After that, they were on their own. I waited around the corner until midnight.

At 11:45, Big G was being escorted by security to the Limo. Allegedly, he provoked a fight with a dude who grabbed his wife to dance. Add alcohol and stupidity rules for some. He was pretty trashed by now and I could see the rest of the crew on their way.

"Take us to the strip club!" is all I heard from the back. "Ladies, are you good with that?" "I want jello shooters" came from Chrissy's lovely lips. "Be there shortly," I said and drove off.

They insisted on me coming in. Annie was working so I said "sure, why not." After letting them out at the front doors, the doors were opened for them and in they went. I pulled around the back and parked the Hummer and made my way to the entrance. Everyone knew me as I went in. Lots of hi Bill's and handshakes along the corridor, after all, I brought many people here for fun.

My group was in the VIP section I had arranged for them on the way over. Several girls came over and then the shooter girl took her place on Big G's lap offering jello shooters from her boobs for everyone. They all took their turn sucking down the jello shooters and acting like lunatics.

Entertaining as it was, I looked around for Annie. Way on the other side I saw my angel grinding on an old dude, doing her job and drawing attention from anyone who could visually see them. She was good I had to admit. I wasn't there to disrupt her work.

Big G had at least two grand in his hands ready to dish out. I told him I would find the best girl in the place and if I did, just tip me well at the end of the night. He said "I'm game." Of course he was, he would probably blow a 4.0 about now.

I was able to get Annie's attention, walked up to her and gave her a huge hug. Big G's eyes lit up. I put my arm around her and her around me and walked back to the VIP area and introduced her.

"Everyone, this is Annie my special friend, take good care of her."
Big G pulled here to his lap and it was on.

Big G called over the management and made a deal to have her and 5
other ladies along with his group of friends, birthday girl and paid for
the larger champagne room for 2 hours. I never saw them until it was
time to leave.

Finally, the Dj played their closing song signifying it was the last
song of the night. Thank God. This is supposed to be a cover job, not
a marathon event. When we reached the Marina Inn and they all
stepped out of the Limo, absolutely everyone hugged me, thanking
me for the great birthday celebration for Chrissy. I said you're
welcome and stepped into the Limo to make sure no wallets, cameras
or phone were left behind and then someone pushed me to the floor.

As I rolled over, Chrissy jumped on me and started grinding on me.
"Woe, I think Jim is waiting for you." She said, "Not really" and then
cameras started flashing and laughter all around us. "Now my
birthday is complete. I can't wait to see facebook in the morning."
Big G was so thankful he tipped me a grand. That's a high roller.

Chapter 12

It was time for another job. The Grinch had sent us a new dossier. This one was close to home. This job is one that I have reservations about. Annie looked at the photo. I knew right away she had seen here before. Pricilla Oakley was considered to be the 'Black Widow'.

She had cleaned out 4 men after marrying them and from the assets she accumulated, paid off the local judges to protect her freedom. The truth is she wasn't innocent and had photos of prominent politicians to use as blackmail if need be.

Annie had been to a fundraiser as a GFE date with a judge a few years back. A little bedroom talk revealed just how powerful this woman was over so many people. She didn't need to hear that but she did. In her business, silence is golden and anonymity will go a long way.

There is a reservation in Annie's voice about this one. She had a secret she wouldn't reveal and it bugged me. We have few secrets from each other and even now the fact that a secret is out there and the other knows about hopefully will never become an issue.

If I didn't know there was one, it certainly wouldn't bother me. From the dossier, like on the news, Ms. Oakley had made a mistake and her 5th husband was tipped off that he was about to be the next victim.

Bobby Oakley was a prominent real estate mogul who managed and owned real estate in 8 states and had interests in the Bahamas and Dubai. His net worth is about 130 million. He believes he has about 3 days to live if he doesn't stop it from happening.

She has used poison, a drunken fall off the yacht, a bogus home invasion and a mugging gone wrong to eliminate her future victims or maybe I should say husbands at the time.

The Grinch upped the ante for Mr. Oakley since it was a rush job. $1.75 million is the cost. Bobby Oakley could easily afford it. $1,000, 000 up front and the balance due upon proof of death were the terms. Annie found out through unique contacts that Mrs. Oakley would be in Charleston early tomorrow and then to the Myrtle Beach Convention Center for a fund raising event, her alibi. Bobby was playing in a charity golf event in North Carolina.

He learned he was supposed to be killed on his way back to Columbia, South Carolina's capital. He didn't have all the details according to the dossier, just the approximate time and method. The plan was a drive by shooting with several cars taking bullets to keep it from looking like he was targeted. A quite a few people will die if this happens.

We had 2 choices. Charleston or Myrtle Beach would be the job's location. Now we had to plan the moment we could get near to her. It had to be done tomorrow leaving us little time to get a detailed plan together.

The pressure was on. To do it at the Marriott in Charleston meant there would be plenty of security cameras in play. It was time to pull out the Harley and get into biker gear. The jean jacket outfit, the wallet on a chain, sunglasses and a scruffy goatee to appear authentic..

Annie loved jumping on the back of the Harley. She would wear her chaps and dress in all leather. She wore a brunette wig that completely changed her look. I corumba. She was absolutely smokin' hot, a real head turner.

We planned on having a rental box truck nearby to stash the bike once we found clearance from any security cameras. There had to be a blind spot somewhere.

When we reached Charleston, after parking behind an abandon storefront, we came rolling around with the Harley and parked it, behind a bus in the Marriott parking lot. We walked to a side door where a well dressed woman was smoking since it's against the rules to smoke inside the Marriott. It's a $250 penalty. We knew what Mrs. Oakley looked like from the dossier and her appearances on television.

Checkout time was about 10 minutes away so we set up camp in the dining area figuring she would be stopping for coffee hoping she didn't already have enough. We could see her driver had pulled up front. Like clockwork she came to grab a coffee.

I had my EOL drug ready for any opportunity. Annie walked up behind her at the ordering counter. I was walking past them when I said, "Hey honey," Annie swung her hand as if to head my way when she caught just enough of her to knock her off balance and then she fell. I immediately came over saying, "I'm so sorry," and gave her a hand pulling up to a standing position.

We offered to pay for her coffee as an apology and she quickly said, "Get away from me bitch, you should watch what you're doing." Annie quickly replied, "I'm so sorry." Before Annie could say another word, Mrs. Oakley said, "Just get away, leave me be."

With that, we stepped back and waited for her to get her coffee and we purchased ours. The waitress asked, "Do you know who that is?" "Not really, who is she?" "That's Mrs. Oakley, the Black Widow" "Really, I think she needs to show some better manners." We smiled at each other and moved on.

When I picked Mrs. Oakley up, I injected the EOL and now the 24 hour countdown is on. We went back to the bike and then back to the truck, secured the bike and headed back to Conway where we rented the truck. What's cool is several bikes were in town cruising, so we kind of blended in. From there, we went straight home, double checking our every move to minimize being noticed.

Our disguise kept any clear image of us incognito from the cameras. We had some concerns about being seen on the bike but with the 24 hour time release of EOL, felt pretty sure we were in the clear.

It was time to meet up with our friends and ride our jet skis in Murrells Inlet. A gorgeous day to be at the beach and a cruise to The Boathouse for some refreshments and later back to Murrells Inlet to store our jet skis.

Chapter 13

Mrs. Oakley had a very busy day preparing for the fundraising event. She was in town to support the pet shelters and acting as MC for the doggie red carpet affair. The event was raising money for the shelters and the promoting of an adoption program to hopefully set new records. Since the economy hit tough times a few years ago around here, the shelters are overcrowded with dogs and cats looking for some love and a new home.

She signed off on the itinerary for the evening. As the crowd settled in and the dogs began prancing around the stage, cameras were capturing some cute and special moments with their handlers.

Only one puppy left a small present that needed to be cleaned up. All in all, 22 pets were adopted that night. Over $5,000 raised and with media coverage that should add to these near record breaking results. Final results will be reported at the end of the weekend.

Mrs. Oakley loved her mimosas and was already on her 6th when she wandered into the lobby to look for a friend of hers. She walked down the hall toward the other events taking place. She caught a smile from 2 young marines who were standing outside one of the events.

The mimosas gave her the courage to approach them, not that she ever feared speaking her mind to anyone. There was something different about their smiles that caught her undivided attention.

The blond haired young man scanned her from top to bottom like he was a TSA scanner and hinted of his enjoyment in what he saw. Mrs.

Oakley was a real looker at 48. Thin, fit, and looked much younger than most her age.

She wore a shimmering dress high up her thighs with red high heeled shoes and bright red lipstick. Can't blame the lads after getting a few days of leave. She was feisty and invited them to er room but said wait about 30 minutes before coming up.

Josh and Jason were stunned and excited at the same time. Apparently, it's been some time since they got laid and tonight was going to be legendary for them. A half hour passed and they began their journey to the elevator and hit the number 12 button. When the elevator stopped, they felt butterflies under their 6 pack abs as they closed in on the room that offered a moment they expected would be unforgettable.

Mrs. Oakley had already changed in to her lingerie and robe. There was no mistaking what her intent was. "Hey boys, pour me a mimosa and have whatever you like and come sit with me." Josh's hands were actually shaking while trying to gain composure and did exactly as she asked. Jason grabbed the bottle of Jack and a cup with ice for his drink of choice.

"Have you boys ever used Viagra before?" "Uhhhhhh, not really but some of the guys say it's awesome." "Well, you're in for a treat tonight. Here's one for each of you." handing it to them. Josh and Jason looked at each other in disbelief and swallowed the pill that would change their young lives.

Before long, the Viagra took effect but by this time, she had both of them kissing and caressing her entire body. Off came the robe and poor Jason nearly died. He had only seen this moment on the internet on his favorite porn sites. "You like?" asked Mrs. Oakley. "Absafreakinlutely!" She offered a devilish grin and said, "Now let's get those clothes off boys."

It took all but about 10 seconds and they stood there fully nude, ready and panting like puppies. "Slowly boys, slowly," she said. That's like telling a fat man to take his time at the buffet.

She put her lips on Josh's and pulled Jason's hands to her breasts. "Don't be afraid boys, I don't bite – MUCH," and then she laughed with a little sarcasm as if to say, you boys have no idea what you got yourself into. Jason slid the teddy off of her and removed her sheer white stockings and gently laid her on the bed. Nice move she thought.

She rolled onto Josh in a 69 position and each did their part to get each other excited. Jason moved on top of her and mounted her from behind which caused Josh to hesitate a moment and took in the pleasure she was unleashing with her sucking lips.

She picked up the pace and in between sucking on Josh, let out serious moans of pleasure. They were all in the moment. Mrs. Oakley choreographed this scenario in her head the minute she saw Jason's eyes checking out her body in the lobby.

She knew the Viagra would keep them going strong since they were young and probably would have lasted 5 minutes tops before losing their hard-ons.

They played with each other for hours and the boys did their part in f@%&ing the crap out of her. Finally spent from sex and alcohol, they laid there and dosed off into la la land. The sun had just come up and all of them were motionless.

They were dead asleep and unresponsive when room service knocked on the door. Josh and Jason's friends had wondered what happened to them since they had not returned to their hotel room yet. They just figured they got lucky or too drunk to make it back. Hopefully they didn't get in a fight and end up in jail.

It was now 11 a.m. and the boys woke up to see the beautiful lady lying in between them. They looked at each other and said, "Dude" "Whoa dude". Not saying another word they dressed and left their Cougar after giving her a soft kiss on the lips, breasts and a gentle brushing of her arms before leaving the room. This was the bewitching hour when the EOL would have caused the heart attack.

Proof of death was delayed. Checking all the news reports, no word on our target, we should hear something soon. Unknowingly, she was still in her hotel room. Stories were on news feeds showing the success of the fundraiser and Mrs. Oakley in all her glory.

Then it came, special announcements hit the news alert on my phone. Mrs. Oakley was found naked and dead in her hotel room. No word of foul play at this time, the police reported. Well, there is my proof of death.

Later that night, speculation was a heart attack brought on by an affair she had been involved in. Two young persons of interest were seen leaving the room on camera. Their identities could not be confirmed until they ran sperm samples and the situation was under investigation. Wow, this was better than I could have planned. Once again, we were in the clear.

Mr. Oakley's lawyer had a private detective put surveillance video in her room. All were amazed at the video once it was reclaimed by the detective. He was pissed and yet a calming satisfaction was seen on his face.

The eventual coroner's report showed a heart attack and she believed it was brought on by the wild sex shown on the video and the news media had a field day with it.

Josh and Jason became rock stars among their fellow comrades after word got out they f&*)ed her to death. Bottom line, we got paid and paid well. Annie and I were ready for a celebration and some alone time. Dinner, a movie and who knows.

Chapter 14

I hated surprises. I like to be in control of my environment and planned most everything I did in advance. That being said, with Annie, some things I had little or no control of. That balance between business and our personal lives seems to be healthy for our working and personal relationship.

My 30th birthday was a day away. It's just another day to me but I could sense something was up. Annie was receiving more text messages than normal and seemed secretive at times. We took in a 7 o'clock movie and I offered to buy some Chinese to take home.

"I'm not really that hungry," I said. "Why not just go home we can cook up a little something on the grill?" "That's what make you so special sweetie, simple and good, I could go for a nice burger."

It was dark so while we were driving home, she put her head in my lap and slid down my shorts enough to pull out my member already at attention. It had been some time since she initiated sex in the car while I was driving.

The last time I nearly crashed into a parked car. She was persistent and I wouldn't say stop or maybe it was I couldn't say stop. It was in her hands literally.

I was so light headed I had to pull over a moment. She had the wildest looking grin on her face. "Wow" is all I could say. You'll get yours later and she gave me that shy little laugh with the head tilted and her finger centered in her lips.

Now drained of fluids, I needed something to drink. A beer would be good about now. As we pulled up to the house, I noticed parking in on Ocean Boulevard was heavier than normal at this time of night.

As I put the key in the lock and twisted it to unlock the door, pushed it open and all at once, "Happy Birthday!" was shouted by about 30 people. I should have known she was up to something, all that secrecy for a reason.

Hugs, kisses and high fives were exchanged as I made my way through the crowd of friends. It was simply awesome to see them all. They had two Hummer Limos on the way and there was no time to waste. "Get me a beer!" I shouted and the night was on.

DJ Eduardo Rush, the top DJ in town was playing music full of high energy and it had everyone pumped up. Conversations were taking place and some were dancing and swaying to the music. It is a very special night indeed.

About midnight, the Hummers arrived. Annie went out to meet the drivers and discussed the agenda for the next 4 hours. She walked back inside and stopped the music. "Hey everyone, thanks for coming and sharing your time with my friend."

We have the limos ready so let's get going," as her voice raised at the end of the announcement. Our friends filed into the Limos and away we went.

We reached the dock waiting on the boat to take us on a cruise. It was a moonlit night and a perfect 70 degrees. Annie stood up on the bar and I noticed she had no panties on under her short skirt. Anyway, I digress. Annie grabbed a microphone and once again thanked everyone for being here and looked at the crowd saying,"Are you ladies ready?"

"Yep," they said in unison. "Let this party begin." On cue, all the ladies yanked off their clothes down to thong bikinis they had on underneath. I didn't think Annie had a thong on. The guys also stripped down to their bathing suits. It was a beach party on the boat.

What's a beach party without a wet t-shirt contest? 4 young ladies with white t-shirts and of course wearing a thong bikini bottom were propped up on a table. I recognized them immediately as 4 of Annie's best friends from the club. They handed me the pressurized water bottle and I began spraying them one at a time.

The crowd voted by cheers and it was a tie in my opinion. Next thing you know, they began kissing and fondling each other. I heard later the captain of the ship nearly crashed the boat when his attention was compromised.

I helped the girls get down from the table and each removed their shirts playing motorboat with my face. The crowd went insane and cheered. "Limo Bill! Limo Bill! Limo Bill!" I bowed before them and once again they started chanting in approval.

It was the best boat ride I could ever remember. Annie had done herself proud. She came over and gave me a birthday kiss to remember with all the onlookers whistling and wooing until she stopped. Does it get any better than this?

After the boat ride was over, we returned to the Limos and back to the house. One of the Limos took those too drunk to drive home from my house and the rest of the party animals left at that time in their cars.

Annie kisses me on the cheek and whispers in my ear, "We're not done yet." "Really? What else do you have planned?" "Let's improvise," is all she would say. She took me by the hand, picked up a black leather bag, and back into the Limo. The driver had his queue and put up the partition. He was given specific instructions from Annie to drive and return in one hour back at the house.

The music was once again set to a high energy level. She reached into her bikini top and pulled out 2 hits of X. We each swallowed it and she said, "Close your eyes honey." I did what she said and Annie placed a blind fold on me. I couldn't see but I heard the zipper on the leather bag open and waited, for what, I had no idea.

She kissed me on the lips with her hands pulling my head to hers in a deep passionate kiss. I was totally turned on at this point. As she moved away she said, "Wait 5 minutes and take off the blindfold."

I heard some metal clank, some heavy breathing and not much else with the music in the background. What in the world was she up to? Annie had put on a leather outfit that included a tight corset, a bra with her huge boobs fully exposed through the holes in the bra. She was naked from the corset down.

She had put shiny steel handcuffs on her wrists behind her back with ankle cuffs attached to each side of the limo leaving her wide open on the floor. She had to do that before handcuffing herself.

I opened my eyes and I had that kid in a candy store look again. OMG. "You never cease to amaze me, if this is my yearly birthday present; I hope I live to be 200 years old." I could tell she approved of my reaction. There was a note hanging from one of her boobs. It said, "I am yours to do as you please. This is about you honey and your imagination, don't let me down."

I removed the note first and began using my lips all over her body. I could tell it affected her immensely by her body language. I reached around her pulling her close to me and began kissing her all over her face and settling in a huge lip embrace.

She let me play her all night long as my imagination went wild. Best birthday present ever.

Time flew by so fast and we arrived back at the house. I stepped out to meet the driver and asked him to wait a minute. I went into the house and grabbed a blanket and approached the limo. "She's not decent so I want to wrap her in the blanket to bring her in."

He just nodded. I reached into my pocket and handed him an envelope with a grand and said,"Thanks man, you were awesome. There's a little extra for any cleaning you might half to do." "Cool," he responded with that "Uh Oh" type of expression.

It was only an hour later and the sun was coming up. I looked at my birthday present one more time.

Now it was time to release her so I undid the handcuffs. She knew she had pleased me big time. I owed for this and I knew it.

Chapter 15

After confirmation of our payment, we destroyed the dossier and counted our blessings that all went well. We had a week without any work lined up so I informed The Grinch we'd be out of town for a while. I had booked us a cruise for a few days and invited her family who she hadn't seen in a few years.

Annie' mom, April, never approved of what she did and her dad, Jack, never knew. It was the family secret. All dad knew was she worked in an office as an executive assistant and as a model part time. Annie's parents lived in San Francisco. Dad had a stroke last year so traveling was not on their normal agenda.

The cruise would be fun and a chance for them to reconnect. We all met at Miami International before boarding the cruise ship. Annie's mom was so glad to see her daughter and ran to hug her. She then gave me a hug and we wheeled dad from the airport for a quick shuttle to the cruise liner. I was Annie's boyfriend for the sake of appearances.

They would never know who I really was and what we actually do unless it was on the news and something went terribly bad. As we boarded, I looked back at the Miami scenery and thought, one day, we'll be far from here. Our bank account has continued to grow over the two years I started my new profession.

The cruise itself was uneventful which for us is highly unusual. Mom and dad had the cabin next to us in case her dad had any problems. His memory was hazy with the onset of Alzheimer's. When we docked in the Bahamas, Annie and I headed to the casino to do a little gambling. We weren't big players but we had fun doing it together. She won, I lost, same old story. Blah, blah, blah.....

It was nice being around her parents and seeing how Annie and her mom interacted. I never had that. My parents were killed in an airplane crash when I was 10. I never fully got over it but learned to accept it and move on.

Through my current connections, I was able to learn a few things about the crash. Most importantly, it wasn't an accident. A terrorist of world prominence was on the plane with my mom and dad.

When the plane landed, he held everyone hostage with a bomb he planned to detonate if his demands weren't met. Long story short, the plane was blown up by a secret attack unit from the UN. The story goes there were 20+ terrorists on the plane and everyone else was collateral damage.

That really sucked hearing the real story if was even real. When I was recruited to be an assassin, I decided early on to avoid collateral damage in any killing. That's the reason I had the EOL drug designed and kept confidential to Dr. Rudi, Annie and myself. Even The Grinch doesn't know exactly how I do it, just that I'm like a ghost or a chameleon that no one ever suspects.

The more I watched Annie, the more I was under her spell. Absolutely everything I want in a woman, she is. I'm sure something could change that but I sure hope not. After her parents returned home, I hugged her and thanked her for being in my life. She started to tear up and just put her head on my shoulder. We just had one of those moments in life you never forget.

Chapter 16

"Hey Limo Bill, have some blackberry moonshine good buddy" Big Dog said with a shit eatin' grin on his face. I took a deep breath and said, "Not while I'm driving but maybe when I come visit you at your job." He wasn't too bright, but wow could he consume alcohol.

If we could win a war with a bet on who could drink the most before passing out, I'd volunteer Big Dog to lead the USA Alcoholic Drinking Team. That's USAADT for short if you want an acronym for a flag to wave in support.

Big Dog and I go way back. His daddy used to bring me along for family outings to the cabin by the lake in VA. I learned how to shoot my first pistol there, lost my virginity to pimple faced Becky, had my first beer and a host of other firsts with Big Dog. His real name is Ben but he's so huge, Big Dog stuck as his nickname. Friends for life as they say.

He brought a few of his redneck friends and some wild women to Myrtle to celebrate Becky's birthday party. Wait a minute Becky is in the limo? Sure enough, the strawberry colored hair young lady had turned into one hell of a looker. Turns out she's a catalog model for Dupers Sporting Goods back home.

They showed me an ad on their phone with her picture and did she ever grow from the pimply little body. "Well Happy Birthday Becky." She looked at me and smiled, "Thanks Mr. Bill". She didn't remember me but I sure did remember her.

They weren't night club kind of people so the decision was to go to bar hopping in the local watering holes in town. We started with Drifter's Bar, the Village Bar and then walked the boardwalk on the water where they fell in love with the one of the boardwalk bars. They made my job easy spending most of the night there. So I thought. Two of the boys got thrown out as I watched them tumbling onto the ground just outside the bar's doors.

Miss Becky shopping somewhere along the boardwalk bought some new clothes and became a sex goddess. She was modeling her new outfit on a table top and her entourage got jealous at all the attention and whistling. The short flowing dress displayed her undercarriage to the wandering eyes in the crowd.

A fight broke out when one fool tried to hug her. Fists were flying, chairs being heaved and the bouncers tossing them into the street. Only Big Dog walked out without being carried. At 500 lbs., there was to be no tossing him anywhere without getting a hernia.

Fortunately they had enough fun for the night and I took them back to their hotel to keep them from getting arrested. Becky was feeling a bit silly and gave me a hug and then started kissing me. My first reaction was to go with it so I did. She pushed me back into the Limo and wanted more.

I looked out the window and saw Big Dog with his arms folded and quickly pushed her to the door and sent her into Big Dog's area. I don't know what that was about and didn't want to know. Time for me to scram. "See ya later Big Dog." "Likewise dude."

Chapter 17

The summer went by rather quickly. Fall golfers were coming to Myrtle Beach and the annual World Golf Competition was getting primed for another 3000 participants. One of my special groups from the western part of Virginia was coming in for their yearly "Crap in the Cup Tour". I mean really, you can't make this stuff up.

The story goes, one morning after an eventful night of record setting drinking (over 400 bottles of beer between 14 guys) one of these idiots crapped in a cup on the first tee and left it there with a message, can you pull the wings off a fly?

A photo of that cup became the center peace for future outings and thus the slogan for their visits. I think I need to revisit the term special in describing them. "Special Needs?" Just saying. Almost her is this year's group of 16, acting like kids in men's bodies, I was just kidding, maybe?

They all arrived in Myrtle Beach at their condos on River Oaks. After unloading everything but their golf clubs and shoes, they didn't even take time to unpack. I had already been summoned to begin transporting them to Bar Insanity nearby.

The first 8 were waiting for me with beers in hand and raising them as I approached their insane looking expressions. They were in rare form having started pounding down the beers for hours during their 5 hour trip to get here. Chants of Limo Bill filled the early evening air and everyone at the pool stopped what they were doing do check out the commotion.

I looked up during my final approach to see the rest of them on their balconies also raising their beers. Those crazy bastards had one dude hanging by his feet as two others held him by the ankles. In true form, he raised his beer in tribute despite seeing the world upside down.

To say this was going to another legendary week is an understatement. When the craziness calmed down, high fives, fist pumps and hugs took place. I looked forward to seeing these guys. I could live my out of body experience of wild times through them. I've done wild things party wise in my life, but I couldn't hold a place next them in any arena. They were icons of crazy to all onlookers.

After loading the first batch into the Limo, we proceeded to Bar Insanity cranking up the hip hop music these 20 thru 40 something's loved to roll with. At first glance Club Insanity seemed like a normal day of business was underway.

Seconds after the first dude got out, Clay; the manager opened the double doors with two buckets of beer and shouted, "What took you so long?" Everyone started laughing; more high fives, a few friendly punches in the gut and the party was on. Inside, hanging above the bar was a banner stating "The 2nd Annual Crap in the Tour" has come to town.

I needed to get back to the condo for the rest of the group and bring them here so off I went. I beeped the horn a few times and they exited the condo and marched straight to the Limo door I had opened for them. They all looked just as they did last year only a little more brazen in attitude. They had planned to get f&^)ed up big time and there is no time like the present.

Pulling up to Bar Insanity again, Clay came out to greet them and they all went inside. There was a section cornered off just for these lunatics. There were buckets of beer filling all the tables. A total of

41 in all and I counted them to verify a record setting night. Each had 5 bottles to a bucket with 205 bottles total. This was in addition to all they drank getting here.

Within minutes, pizzas and a variety of wings were added to the feast. If you need to get away from everyday life, this is how you do it. At least that was part of their plan. They should be party coaches but I doubt their students would keep up. There was plenty of reminiscing, laughter, whistling, howling, sarcastic jokes, picking on the new guy in the group and so on. This behavior was expected picking right where they left off last year.

The cute waitresses were playful with all their comments and from time to time, these guys would make it rain like they were in a strip club after getting them on top of a table and having them dance Coyote Ugly style.

After a while, several of them wandered over to the pool tables, with buckets of beer in hand and wagering a little to add to the fun. Others mingled with the bar crowd and shook hands with perfect strangers making new friends and hitting on the ladies by offering free beers and stealing hugs even if they were pushed away, it didn't deter them. They had an excuse. They were acting like idiots with a smile and who could turn that down?

The office had called me to pick up another group of golfers from the airport. I had to leave for a while, I explained to them, but I'll be back. At the airport, I tracked the flight number to a plane coming in from Atlanta and it was hitting the ground in 2 minutes.

To my surprise, it was 4 ladies who had a ton of luggage with their clubs. They were in their 50's but all very attractive. We loaded up and arrived at the Marriott Grand Dunes. The valet assisted in gathering all the luggage and clubs to take to their rooms after check in. Marie, the loveliest of them all, was a friend of the resort's manager.

VIP treatment was promised for these ladies. They didn't act anything other than appreciative and professional for my services. I wish more people were like that.

My phone rang and it was Annie. "Hey honey, how are you doing?" She said, "I'm bored." It was a Tuesday and I usually only work the weekends like her. She had already heard about my wild group of golfers and asked me how it was going with them.

"They are an insane bunch, but lots of fun. How would you and some of the girls like to hang out at Bar Insanity tonight and meet the guys?" I said. "Sure, why not. I'm bored so what the hell." "Make some calls and I'll be by the house soon to pick you up." "Perfect she said," and hung up.

By the time I made it home, she had dressed in her voluptuous outfit she normally wore at the club. Bridgette, Molly, Electra who was back in town to visit and a few more dancers were off and others joined this entourage of beauty. We had to make several stops to collect them all and finally we were on our way.

I got a call from Eddie. "A few of the guys want to go the strip club tonight." I responded, "How about I bring some of my friends to you tonight and save the strip clubs for later in the week." Eddie asked, "Are they hot?" I said, "I think so but I'll let you guys be the judge of that." "Great, how soon?" "About 15 minutes work?" "Cool man, you're the best."

Annie sat up front with me while I drove the Limo with one hand on the wheel and the other caressing Annie's boobs. Her low cut dress made it so tempting and easy. When I pulled up to Bar Insanity again, I asked the ladies to wait a couple of minutes until I came back to open the door. I told them I had a plan in mind. Everyone agreed.

I gathered the guys for a huddle. "This night gentlemen will be a very special night for you to remember. For the married guys, you will test your marriage vows. If you have a girlfriend, you will be tested too. If you are single, you may never see a woman live up to what you are about to experience. So are you ready for a new friendly experience of a lifetime?"

You could see the anticipation and puzzlement on their faces. "Well hell ya!" "OK then, I want you all to line up single file along the bar stools and be ready to greet some of my friends." They all thought this was strange but went along with my directions.

I went back to the Limo and waited about another 5 minutes letting the guy's anticipation build and then one by one they exited the Limo. Traffic stopped in the parking lot, a few guys fell over the potted plants outside and I then opened the door to Bar Insanity.

"Guys, I want you to meet my friends," as the beauties entered the bar. They all looked at each other in shock and Eddie shouted, "Limo Bill, you are a Rock Star." I laughed and introduced the ladies one by one and then the guys.

"This is Eddie, Jake, Josh, Sammy, Johnny, Stephen, Sean, Harold, Mikey, Big Dick Dave, Cameron, Robbie, Mark, Frank, Jeremy and Psycho Billy." "And guys, this is Annie my special lady friend responsible for everyone here tonight." Big Dick Dave shouted, "Hail to Annie!" and the place broke out into cheers. All the other patrons joined in too.

In no time, guys at every table were on the phone texting and calling their buddies up to say get over here now. Business at Bar Insanity that night set record highs in sales volume and alcohol consumption. Da!

Chapter 18

The fun was interrupted by a message from The Grinch. He had a new job for me to complete in a hurry. He was sending me the dossier with specific instructions concerning the message and to let me know it was being sent.

I got Annie's attention and told her I was going home to get the details off the computer and I'd be back. She assured me the party would go on for some time and her friends were having a blast themselves.

All was good at the bar leaving me the opportunity to get up to speed on our next job. It's never anything personal for me but I dread the day I might know one of the targets. This wasn't one of them.

Jim Bogatti was my new target. He was a thief, a murderer and all around bad guy. He used his muscle to build his real estate fortune. He would target neighborhoods up and down the east coast he knew would fetch a solid return on investment. Some people say he would simply buy their property but always at a major discount.

Others he would escalate crime in the neighborhood to entice people to move away and with the stubborn ones he would use death threats and vandalism to devalue the property and increase a need for them to move out.

He had people to do this so he came in looking like a savior and built new communities and shopping centers in these stolen neighborhoods. Like most businessmen of greed, he did one too many and had an apartment building destroyed by explosives. It was supposed to be vacant of all tenants but a few refused to give in.

It turns out, Ella and Crystal Richards were in the building and perished in the explosion. Ella and Crystal were the daughters of Richards' Equity and Investment Funds traded on Wall Street and worth $48.9 Billion. Their dad, Dan Richards took this very personal.

He reached out to our service through secretive channels and needed to deny any connection should anything go wrong. That's why they contacted us. Our reputation is undoubtedly the most sought after assassin service with a perfect resume of success. No one who contacts us is ever disclosed.

If Bogatti thought he had power, he hadn't met a man of Richards' wealth and power. Michelle Bogatti, Jim's wife was the woman behind the man creating havoc in the rise of their organization. She pulled the strings for her puppet husband, the face of their empire. If anyone doubts this, have a conversation with any of the employees or attend a board meeting.

With the information in Bogatti's dossier, we found a couple of weaknesses to exploit. Our challenge, one I'm not a fan of is we have been commissioned for a double kill. Both the husband and wife must be eliminated. It's much riskier to make two heart attacks look random and not appear as natural. I was actually surprised they commissioned this job to me.

The good news is the payoff is worth it. The job is worth $2 million for both plus an undisclosed thank you from Dan Richards according to The Grinch. All I know is we have a job to do and plan for and I had my wild group of friends in town.

Annie and I got to work right away. Myrtle Beach has many properties in short sell and bankruptcy due to the economy. Although many areas around the country have recovered to some degree, Myrtle is a little behind the curve although better times are projected real soon.

After plenty of research, we found a segment of land available that would be an easy acquisition for his style of investing. I had a good realtor friend start a rumor that would get the Bogatti's attention. A special invitation was sent to Michelle showing all the details of the property.

The one business many locals keep hoping for is to have some casinos in Myrtle and surrounding areas. There are many large parcels to build a casino on. The old mall that was knocked down many years ago is one. Another parcel is where the failed amusement park has there remnants still in place. Still another is where the old Pavilion sat right on the ocean.

Finally with all the older hotels getting old and out of date, statistics suggest replacing them could bring a better clientele to Myrtle Beach, it opens the option of replacing those hotels with modern hotels and resorts connected to a casino. It'll never be Vegas but it would offer year round revenue streams and jobs the local economy could use.

Jim has his own Cessna and figured he'd fly him and his wife in to check out the details and survey the property. They made plans to visit in 2 days leaving me an opportunity to inject the EOL within 24 hours of their return trip. I had Annie reconfirm their itinerary explaining she was my assistant and welcomed them to Myrtle and offered to arrange an overnight stay at a resort of their choice.

What I had hoped for came true. They were flying in strictly to check things out and return shortly after having dinner. Annie said, "Great, I'll make the dinner arrangements around 6 before make your return trip." "Thank You", said Michelle. With that, they both hung up. In her conversation with Michelle, she was able to get their arrival and departure time plus their landing location.

This meant I had to somehow get to him by tomorrow morning before 11 a.m. He stored his plane in Maryland at a small airport near BWI. I had hoped to meet him somewhere I could get close to him.

Doing anything at the airport could cause suspicion after the fact. Annie did some quick digging and fortunately found out he had planned to play golf tomorrow morning in Bowie. She luckily booked us as a twosome to tee off 30 minutes after Jim Bogotti.

We quickly scrambled and got on the road for the 8 hour trip over night. We looked at each other and both were thinking the same thing. Maybe a little hanky panky on the road trip? Smarter heads prevailed knowing there would be time for that later. We made it to Bowie about 6 a.m. Found a small diner to grab some breakfast and to get ready for meeting Bogotti.

To make sure, we didn't miss our chance, we showed up at the country club early enough to go to the driving range with a view of everyone entering the clubhouse. This proved to be fruitful because just as we were finishing the bucket of balls, a Limo approached the bag drop area and Bogotti stepped out with his golf shoes already on.

The driver popped the trunk and the valet took the clubs and placed them on the rack in preparation to putting them on his personalized golf cart. A giant emblem of a golf ball in green with the lettering, JB in the center placed on the sides and front of the cart.

Bogatti's buddies all shook hands and made sarcastic comments about him being here. He had jabbing answers for a few of them and they all had a good laugh. Already, they were discussing the format for their wagering system. By this time I started to look for an opportunity to get close to him.

Annie met me inside at the snack counter and I ordered two coffees and grabbed a donut. He noticed my beautiful partner and came walking toward us. I had already prepared for the handshake to dispense the EOL drug into Bogotti's system. He reaches Annie's hand and kissed it gently and introduced himself, "Hello, I'm Jim and who might you be."

She played coy and with a shy smile, said, "Daffny, aren't you the gentleman." His smile was now as big as house. "Hello" as I shook his hand," I'm Dr. Talbert and I see you've met my assistant." "Assistant what? He asked.

It was too easy make a suggestive joke right then so I stayed cool and answered him with, "Well, that depends on how much I'm paying her." That leaves plenty for Bogatti's own interpretation and we all started laughing. At that point I reached into my pocket and forced my phone to fake ring. "This is Dr. Talbert" I pretended to listen to someone talking. "Oh, seriously Monica, I'm about to tee off."

More pretend listening. "I can be there in 40 minutes, get me Dr. Walker." "I apologize for having to leave but we have to go immediately." He reached into his pocket and offered a business card saying. "Call me sometime and we'll hit a few around." "Sure, I'd like that and turned to the door with Annie following me.

It would be a long trip back but it was time to get on the road. Before we left last night we did stop by the bar to say hey and let the guys know we had a birthday party to attend and that we'd catch up with them tonight. Looking at my watch, I called Nathan, the other Limo driver to pick them up tonight, same as last night.

Chapter 19

Traffic sucked on the way back but we persevered and made it back by midnight. I took Annie back to her place and took off for Bar Insanity and the guys. We had accomplished what needed to be done today. Created some cover, delivered the EOL at the right time and made it back all in 24 hours.

When I walked in, you would have thought I was a true star of some type. "Limo Bill, Limo Bill, Limo Bill!" the chants kept coming. There were buckets of beer and wings everywhere and most were shitfaced at this point in the night. It was about midnight. I was beat but I held my own and grabbed a beer and joined the conversations while the ball game was on. The guys playing pool were in no better condition.

"What time is tee time tomorrow?" "11 a.m., are you joining us?" Robbie said. "If I do, I'll have to leave early. I had a long night last night at the birthday party," and smiling I said "and afterwards," leaving my night with Annie up to their imagination. Of course, all I did was drive a friggin' car for 8 hours. I needed to make an investment for emergencies going forward.

About 6 beers later, I had Nathan take me home. That bed felt like a cloud after the last 24 hours. The alarm went of at 10 and to the shower I went. I was determined to meet up with them at the course, thus adding to my cover from the job.

As we teed off, the EOL should be doing its deed and all would be righted. If not, they would be arriving in Myrtle while I'm playing golf. The third hole was magical. As we waited on the group ahead of us to finish out the hole before we teed off, the sound of a small plane was coming in our direction.

Big Dick Dave pointed up to the sky and in the near distance we watched a small plane struggling to stay in the air. In seconds, it came crashing down on the other side of the bridge where we couldn't see. A puff of smoke billowed from behind the bridge.

I'm thinking Bingo if this was the Bogatti's who had crashed. We continued on to tee off and of course the talk was all about the plane until Josh bombed a shot straight toward the greed. He almost landed the green on a short par 4. We all bowed and clapped for him. Best shot I've ever seen him do considering he had a snowman on the first hole.

The anxiety was getting to me. I started checking my phone of news alerts but nothing yet. After we completed the ninth hole, I headed to the snack counter. Ordered a hot dog with onions and mustard and took notice of the TV in the eating area. At the bottom of the screen, a news alert was rolling across the bottom of the screen.

A Cessna had crashed in near Rt. 501. There are no know survivors and identities have still not been confirmed. They did say the plane was from the Maryland area. My assessment was this was the Bogatti's plane. I just needed it to be confirmed. I called Annie to have her update me once confirmed.

"Guys, I'm buying today. Beers for all whole 4 foursomes and whatever they want to eat. Here's $300 I told the waitress, keep the change." She smiled and said, "You got it" and began taking orders. I was taking the place of Harold. Apparently he overdid it last night was left behind today.

We were on the 18th hole when Annie called. "I was about to call you, what's the latest?" "It is confirmed, the Bogotti's bit the dust.

Great news, ha?" "Oh ya! That makes my day so far. I'm heading home shortly, have you got time to come over?" "Sure, just give me about an hour." The first thing I did was grab a bottle of wine and sink into the hot tub. It felt great to relax.

After a quick dip in the pool, I laid on the stretched out lounge chair and taking in some sun before it goes down. I barely heard Annie come in, but I knew it was her. She has this walk I know belongs just to her. "Hey honey, do I need to bring a glass?" "Nope, got one here just for you."

She gently kissed me on the lips upside down and made her way to the hot tub. I actually missed her lately. We've been so busy even though she was with me; I still missed her touch, her sweet sounds. I joined her in the hot tub. We kissed for short while and she sat on my propped up legs running her arms around my neck.

I was lucky, truly lucky to have such a true friend, a partner to share my life with. We were more in tune with each other than most married people we knew. Despite our crazy secretive and portrayed cover lives, we knew we had a good thing going.

We moved our private moment inside while beach goers were exiting the beach as the sun was going down. With wine in hand, we stared into each other's eyes, smiled and after taking a sip of wine and putting the glasses down, progressed into a deep hug. Our passion was heating up.

These are always moments to die for. I removed her top and kissed her neck multiple times getting little reactions from her every time I removed my lips. Slowly, I moved to her breasts and pierced nipples. The passion kept building and we went horizontal on the couch.

Annie was on top and me with my back to the black leather fabric. She removed my tank top and returned the kissing I did on her to my neck and chest. Then she brought her boobs to my lips for some more foreplay. She had magnificent boobs. Well paid for and magnificent.

Finally we were totally nude and she twisted until we were in the 69 position. Without missing a beat, our lips reached the appropriate targets and our passions went out of control.

I said, "Baby, I think you deserve a massage from the master." She said with a sexy tone, "Really, the master? Well master Bill, you're on." I slid out from underneath her and grabbed some lotion. I was always a fan of the aroma of cucumber melon when giving massages, strawberry and coconut were also good choices.

I poured some on to my hands and very methodically, began messaging her neck and shoulders, a deep rub for a deep result. Next, I messaged her back and hips, moving up and down multiple times alternating the pressure each time. Some small karate chop style movements over her entire back and then the finger nail scraping motion down her back.

Being very gentle though, it would just add a sensation to her skin along with the lotion. Next was her ass and what an ass. I didn't know whether to eat her buns or massage them. I kept in the moment and added lotion to her ass and legs down to her ankles.

I repeated all the same motions from the top half of her body to the bottom half. The final move meant adding more lotion to my hand and rubbing the rest of her.

She was getting really horny by now and so was I. It was time for her to roll over. Starting with the neck, I made all the same massaging moves with added attention to her magnificent breasts. By the time I reached her ankles, she was royally turned on. The intensity rose as I entered her and made love with a passion level of 20 on a scale of 10.

She smiled at me and brought my hand to her most sensitive region and together, we enjoyed the moment when she exploded. "F^$% Ya!" I exclaimed. She laughed so hard we both fell onto the floor and stayed in a wonderful embrace for a good while.

It was time to pick up the guys in the Limo. I don't know how, but they just keep on keepin' on. When I arrived at their place, we didn't fill the Limo up this time. 4 of them had wimped out and were nearly brain dead from alcohol. I've certainly seen this before.

They needed a night off. One of them had a few joints to celebrate the night before getting in the Limo. The aroma and squinty eyes gave it away for those who participated. Look out for munchies time my friends. Clay was there to greet them upon arrival. It was steak night and no one left hungry.

This was strip club night. Some of these good ole boys don't get out much so after pounding down the beers, eating some grub and more razzing each other from today's golf, they were ready to put a scare into some new faces.

Their annual choice was The GFE Gentleman's Club. In this exclusive club, the dancers sport a fully nude revue in a separate room by invitation only. This can be trouble but we'll see. We loaded the Limo up with coolers of beer and arrived after a speed beer drinking half hour ride.

At the club, going through the security scanner is like watching a clown show. Every time the buzzer sounds, someone has a sarcastic comment. It took 15 minutes to get them all through and by now the line was out the door. They picked a group of tables to set up house and their night was now a new story for future telling.

I left them there to fend for themselves. I needed a break so I went out to the Limo to relax for a moment. Besides, the non smoking rule doesn't apply here and it gets so thick, I could hardly breathe after 10 minutes. I went back in about an hour later to check on them.

There was Jeremy, Eddie, Josh, Jason, Scott and Big Dick feeding ones by the twos to the dancers as they came around the stage to where they were. The rest of the group was either in the private rooms or were being entertained with lap dances. I give them an hour and hell will break loose somewhere with this crew.

I returned to the Limo and about 30 minutes later, sure enough, four huge bouncers in black had Jeremy and Josh by their armpits raised off the ground and escorted out the doors. Allegedly, they tried to put 20's into the girl's in some inappropriate places and were spotted by the bouncers. They claimed they asked first. Ya, right?

Add alcohol and stupidity occurs. All in all, it took about 45 more minutes to get them all out and into the Limo. One of the dudes fell in lust and gave his last week's pay check trying to get laid. What was he thinking?

Chapter20

Finally the autopsy was back about the Bogatti's. A heart attack caused Jim Bogatti to crash the plane with his wife, Michelle, aboard the plane. The Grinch said Mr. Richards, who was still grieving over his losses, appreciated our services so much that he added an extra mil to the payment. That was the special thing he was talking about. The Grinch wired $2.4 million to our account.

Time for a little time off and a little celebration for Annie and I. The golfers had returned home so I surprised Annie with a trip to Aruba. We both informed work, it was vacation time and we'd be back in a couple of weeks. When Bridgette heard the news, she was jealous and wanted to come.

I said, "Tell you what, I'll leave 2 tickets at reservations and for her to bring a friend of her choice for the second week we are there. The first week is ours, agreed?" Annie gave me a wild passionate kiss and said, "Love it but I ain't telling Bridgette until later, I might want you all to myself for two weeks." "I love it when you take control, my crazy and lovely bitch," I added.

Annie informed the Grinch and her job of our plans and we were free to do whatever. We have enough money earned to retire for life already but we're too young to do nothing so for a few more years the plan is to continue our lives as they are. It keeps the excitement and spice in our lives every single day.

Annie wasted no time packing a few bags, mostly bikinis, Victoria Secrets lingerie and short dresses, shorts and shoes. Lots of shoes. I told her to go easy, we'll be shopping in Aruba plus I had a surprise waiting for the day after we arrived. She took the hint and cut her list in half. Now that made sense I told her. She always liked my surprises.

The Limo arrived as scheduled to take us to the airport. Nathan came up to the door to retrieve the luggage and load them into the trunk. I told him to have a bottle of champagne iced for the trip to the airport. We were off to a great weekend in Aruba.

Along the way, we shared a romantic moment or two enjoying the champagne. "A toast to my beautiful and loving partner, I am so glad I have you to share my most special moments with," and then I put my glass to hers. "Here, here honey," she said appreciating my toast.

She raised her glass again, "and a toast to a hunk of a man who continually keeps me wanting more out of life with him." Well, that's it. It's a consensual commitment to keep the fire burning and see where our lives take us together.

We passed the Myrtle Beach Airport and she said, "Hey what's going on? We just passed the airport." Nathan turned his head and smiled at her. She turned to look at me a little puzzled. I looked at her and said, "We've worked so hard lately, I made a little investment in preparation for Aruba and our future." "OK" she hesitantly said.

We proceeded to the corporate commercial airport just around the corner and Candy was there to meet us. She shook our hands and said, "I'll be piloting the jet with Buzz for your trip to Aruba." "Honey, this is our new jet. I hope you approve," I said. "Really, absolutely, you never stop amazing me sweetheart."

A voice comes over the speakers, "This is the captain speaking. Relax and enjoy your flight. We should be in Aruba in a little less than 3 hours. The weather in Aruba is 77 and sunny." Candy sounded very professional. It's the name that get's both of us considering Annie's cover profession. There was a Murphy bed in this jet in case we had a very long flight to like Australia or someplace.

Also in case we wanted to remain up to date members of the mile high club. Around the bed was sliding partitions for privacy. Our flight attendant was a very red headed young woman named Veronica. "Please bring us some champagne and some strawberries 'n cream Veronica." "Right away sir…" Wow, sir…

We couldn't resist. As soon as the champagne, strawberries and cream arrived, we quickly tested the sliding partition. Perfect I thought. Opening the Murphy bed, we brought our goodies and feasted like a king and queen.

I opened the partition a hair and asked Veronica for another bottle of champagne. When I opened the second bottle, Annie got really frisky and removed everything except her thong. I joined in the activities and did the same. Well, no thong so I was completely naked.

With her finger, she motioned me to the bed. I looked at her as to say who me, and moved toward where she was sitting on the edge of the bed. For the next 30 minutes, we caressed every in of each other's bodies as foreplay. When the foreplay ended, our excitement hit new heights.

The good part about being young, I soon regained my enthusiasm and we enjoyed round two. We christened our new toy and named the jet "Wild Insanity." We made a pact to do this often on a vacation trips we use the jet for. Like I'm gonna say NO.

Time sure flew as we scurried to get dressed after the announcement until we were decent. We slid the panels back and put up the Murphy bed with a note – 'Please clean the sheets before the next liftoff'.

Annie whispered to Veronica, "I was naughty, please have the sheets cleaned." Veronica smiled walking away.

This was going to be awesome.   7 days with no distractions, especially not work or so I thought.   The Grinch was aware of our location and sure enough, he commissioned a job right here in Aruba. You dirty dog you.   The targets name was Phil Newman.

Newman was an arms dealer who scammed one our clients out of 6 million dollars worth of weapons.   Basically, it was 3 specially designed hand held missiles that you could not only program coordinates for a large hit but it could split into 4 smaller missiles if programmed to and take out 4 separate smaller targets like a house, car office or whatever and it is worth 2 million each on the black market.

The firing weapons were supposed to come with 5 bombs each for the 2 mil.   They were never delivered as scheduled.

The dossier would be sent to us by satellite to our encrypted computer by tomorrow.   Newman was expected in Aruba in 3-4 days to do some gambling at a high stakes poker game in a private location near the casino.

When I informed Annie, she at first looked bummed and then turned her attitude around quickly and she headed out shopping.   I might have to take up shopping if it's that easy to be happy I thought.

I took a walk to the beach and lay on one of the hammocks.   The breeze was sensational and the view extraordinary.   Bikini babes rolling their behinds as they walked by and if that wasn't enough, the ocean was so calm and blue. A waiter came up to me asking if I would like a drink and said sure. He returned with a tropical drink with an umbrella and a shot of tequila. I'm set now.

When I made it back to the room, Annie was wearing a new sexy outfit that hardly contained her sweet boobs. I wasn't complaining, I'm just saying. "Let's go to the casino," she said. "Good idea honey, what do you plan to wear?"

"This and my silver bikini bottoms," she said. "That works for me." She grabbed her clutch and out the door we went. We were staying at the Marriott which had this cool circle on the ground level where a small boat would pick up and drop off depending where you were going.

The captain taxied us to a spot near the casino and we walked from there. Inside the casino, the traditional casino type slot machines were everywhere. Near the front they had wagering on race tracks from around the world. Sports' betting was also available with Jai Alai, it was a sport I've seen once live in Florida, you bet on it too.

I let her do her thing and watched all these people acting like lunatics trying to win the big one. I moved to the black jack table and took my position there. It was a $1,000 table. I bought $10,000 in chips to start. My first hand and I was spoiled. Ace Ten, BLACKJACK.

The dealer had 20 (two picture cards). This went on for about 15 minutes and I lost it all. Plenty of more money to lose where that came from. I could see Annie playing the slots. She looked like she was having a blast so I let her be.

Chapter 21

Since the possibility existed our vacation could be interrupted tomorrow, I had my surprise for Annie moved up to tonight. It was important we started off the vacation with a bang. I had a arranged for a fashion show in our penthouse suite. Nearly a dozen of the top businesses in Aruba had signed on and sent their best products. It was scheduled for 9 p.m. I needed to get Annie back to the hotel in time.

When I went back to the casino, she had a bucket full of silver dollars. She won about $750 to this point. I snuck in behind her and started kissing her neck as I wrapped my arms around her. "Time for your surprise honey," I softly whispered in her right ear. Then I moved to nibble on her left ear and whispered, "They're coming."

"What?" "You'll see, just follow me," I whispered one last time. I picked up her bucket full of coins, took her by the hand and made our way to the Marriott and our room. As the door opened, she was taken by surprise with all the people in the room.

I sat her on a royal antique chair brought in just for the event. "My dear, this is your very own fashion show and it's time to shop," as I bowed and swung my hand from left to right pointing to the first fashion displayer. The anticipation was killing her.

First up were some very colorful types of clothing. With island music playing in the background, the beautiful native models brought one dress after another, wearing sexy shoes I knew she would love. She pointed to the outfits she liked and wanted every pair of shoes. "Slow down my lady, plenty more to look at," I told her.

The next set of models, had jewelry to display. They had rings, a multitude of necklaces, earrings, and ankle bracelets in diamonds. Even a chain that was made of silver and went around the waist and rested on the hips was on the models.

Next, models sported some incredible hats of all designs. Another model had some very fashionable scarves and on and on. She had selected more than a few bags of luggage could hold. The very last group of models came out and Annie's eyes lit up. They were assorted fashion pieces from the world of bondage.

Shiny red ball gags with intricate head straps, various types of blindfolds, a leather body outfit from head to toe, chains, cuffs, leather straps, leather corsets, whips in hand and many other toys they could experiment with. Rolls of vinyl tape, nipple weights and suction cups, dildo's and items I don't even want to describe.

When I added this to the show, I had no idea this would be available. I figured a few toys and that would be it. Later I learned they had a store on the internet and lots of inventory. I asked the vendors to pack up anything Annie didn't choose and we can negotiate a price for her favorite choices.

After all this was completed and a deal worked out and paid for, all the vendors left us. Annie came over and jumped up on me with her legs around my hips and my hands holding her up as I grabbed her ass.

It was getting late but she went and grabbed a few toys to get the night rolling. She liked choosing her own toys and I had no reason to complain. She grabbed a vibrator and an outfit consisting of leather. Annie began pulling on a tight pair of leather shorts over the vibrator and added a leather bra.

She handed me the remote control. "You naughty little woman," I said and watched her slide her teasing tongue seductively across her red lipsticked lips. She handed me 3 rolls of tape and said, "Be creative." I started wrapping tape around her wrist behind her back and finally ended by the shoulders. Her arms were completely encased in the tape. With the little tape left, I wrapped it around her eyes as a blindfold.

She was my playmate for the night. I had the remote and used it judiciously. It was a fun method of foreplay she liked. With her arms bound, she would get super excited until I would remove them for a ravishing love making session.

After removing all the bonds, we each took a nice hot shower. Relaxed and spent, we finally went to sleep. I had wild dreams that night. I found myself on a plane on the way to Aruba with the sexiest woman alive, visited a casino, had bondage sex and then I woke up. Wow, it wasn't a dream. I looked over at all the bondage toys lying on the floor near the bed.

Chapter 22

In the morning, we received the file for Newman. He was a bad dude. He killed dozens of his customers just because he didn't trust them. Usually kept the money and this wasn't the first time he didn't deliver as promised.

Eliminating him would give justice to many other militants and countries who had used his services. I'm not sure if that's a good thing or bad thing. Annie and I met with a certain contact on the island that The Grinch had set up for us. I was to meet him on a safari trip around the island. The island is about 25 miles in circumference.

The volcano built island turned out to be a dream vacation for so many. In our travels, Annie and I saw multi colored houses and the neighborhoods the poor locals lived. Dogs walked the streets looking undernourished as well as some of the kids.

On our 8 passenger jeep, we had an Italian family join us on the back but didn't speak any English. Yadol pulled me aside at one of the stopping points to check out the ancient relics. He informed me of Newman's previous visits and habits.

The casino was definitely the place to meet him. Yadol helped arrange a seat for me at the private poker game. He said to make sure you have at least $500,000 U.S. to enter the game with. I had my money wired to me and I had 2 days before the big game.

I joined a small poker game just to get my face shown before the big game. I figured a little presence was a good thing. I lost most of the 10 grand I brought to the game so the word would get out I might be an easy mark. It worked and I was a loser when it came to gambling anyway.

We continued on to the back side of the island and the waves were crashing hard against the rocks. It has been suggested this is where the young lady who disappeared may have been disposed of. If I found the killer, he'd be getting a dose of EOL just because.

There were no cruise ships or ships of any type within view in this area. The current is so strong, most ships wouldn't survive I was told. We waved to the Italian family and they jumped back in the back seats of the jeep. As I steered the jeep through the rocks and crevices, it got quite bouncy and when I looked back at them, they were bouncing up and down holding on tight.

I slowed to ask if they were ok. They didn't understand me and were smiling and laughing. Clearly they were having a good time. I tried to explain things with my hands but they responded talking in Italian with rapid hand movements. I gave up and smiled. Our journey was soon over.

Annie and I dressed for dinner at Texas de Brazil, a Brazilian style steakhouse. Our cab was outside ready to take us. When we entered, we were pleased to meet some folks who spoke American. Dinner conversation was a little dramatic with everyone trying to top the other's story. Our cards were Green for Go and a different skewer of meet was presented to each person on the table in rotation.

There was Filet Mignon, pork, chicken, fish and a salad bar the size of a city with sushi and more goodies. Finally we were stuffed. We turned the card over to Red and paid our bill. When we made it back to the Marriott, a fireworks show had started with dancers and fire acrobatics. It was awesome.

The poker game was about to begin. Annie and I met Yadol at the casino. Annie brought her bucket of silver dollars and Yadol lead me through some tall doors made of gold. Behind the doors, Neman and 4 other players were milling around in preparation for the high stakes game.

A gorgeous tall slender woman in a long red dress with slits on the sides for the flesh of her legs to peek in and out of as she moved, collected our briefcases of money and in return, handed each of us a box of poker chips equaling the half million in our suitcases. This was a winner takes all stakes game. The winner ends up with a cool $2.5 million.

$10,000 was the ante per hand. The cards were then dealt. 7 card stud was the game of choice for tonight. Before we started playing, I shook the hand of Newman with a firm grip wishing him luck. The EOL was injected at that moment and the clock was now ticking.

I quickly removed the drug. The dispenser showed green. I moved it to my other hand and shook all the other players' hands. Newman was a pro and won the first two hands. From that point on we took our turns folding, bluffing and winning hands. Reading the body language in the room was challenging.

I was the second person to go broke and sat around watching the final 3 challenge each other. They all stayed in for over an hour before I excused myself and wished them farewell and good luck. I found out from Yadol that Newman went all in holding a full house, kings high.

His opponent held 4 5's and took home the huge prize. Newman kicked the chair across the room, storming out pissed he lost. That was the last we saw of him. The winner did spend some winnings on 4 women to visit Newman in his room as a consolation. He probably would have been killed without the gesture. Newman probably will still have him killed anyway.

The next morning, Newman was gone and we continued on to our vacation plans. Annie had increased her winnings to over $1,100. It hardly made up for my losses but I didn't care. Her winnings will make her more fun to be with which I found out later. The good news is the half million I lost to perpetrate the assassination would be reimbursed after the kill is confirmed.

Chapter 23

Annie's friend Bridgette was to be here soon. She used the extra ticket to bring Molly who she has had intimate relations with in the past. The term girlfriends have a loaded meaning for them. Annie and I spent the day on the beach and later in the Jacuzzi in our room.

When her friends arrived, we planned on a night of partying in our suite and a tour of the island and some snorkeling. All the preparations for a private yacht had been handled by Yadol. He was my concierge/informant I really appreciated having around. I had a few more needs for him to handle before the girls arrived.

We met Bridgette and Molly at the airport. It was like watching models on the cat walk when they strutted out the doors with their bags being wheeled by the valet. We picked them up it the safari jeep we kept on rental. It brought wide smiles from the girls and Annie met them with a big hug. I hugged them as well assisting them into the jeep. The bags were secured and we drove to the Marriott.

The penthouse had 4 bedrooms leaving plenty of space for them to join us. After catching up for a couple of hours, we ordered room service. I ordered like it was a buffet. A plate of nearly everything on the menu was ordered along with a case of champagne and wine with plenty of ice plus a bottle of tequila for shots.

A knock on the door and Yadol entered. "Here is the items you asked for Mr. Bill." "Thank you Yadol, you're the best, dude." I put the bag to the side and opened a couple bottles of champagne and wine.

"A toast to by best friend Annie and her best friends" I began. We all raised our glasses and we all said, "Cheers," as we took a drink. Annie chimed in, "A toast to living life to its fullest ever day with my best friends." Again, "Cheers!" from all of us and we took a drink. Bridgette smiled and said, "A toast to Annie and Bill for inviting us to share life with them."

We all raised our glasses again, "Cheers," as we took yet another drink. Molly said, "Now it's my turn, A toast to everyone in the room, let's crank this party up," as her voiced rose to a screaming voice and we finished our glasses of champagne ready for more.

We always had fun times together and this should prove to be no different. After reloading all the champagne glasses, we stood up and raised our glasses until they all touched. As soon as the chiming stopped, the group gulped the whole glass down.

I clicked the remote and the music filled the room. A little more volume and we had our own night club for 4. Bridgette wasted no time and poured shots and handed each of us a shot and a slice of lime. We all drank our poison, bit the lime and made funny faces.

I picked up the bag to see what Yadol had brought me, nice, a dozen joints of the finest mary-g-wanna on the island. When the girls saw the pot, shouts of joy overrode the music. We lit the first one and passed it around.

The effects didn't take long with the shots and champagne. Everyone seemed too happy. Da! After about an hour, the room service I ordered earlier came in handy. Munchies time was on full alert. With all the choices, everyone found more than one of their favorite foods.

The wine kept flowing and the pot smoking kept going too. The mood was mellow and everyone couldn't stop smiling. The room was filled with smoke and since none of us smoked cigarettes, the aroma was very specific.

I took another look in the bag and I found 10 hits of X and a dozen purple pills. Bridgette's curiosity brought her over to check out the goodies. "I want one, I want one!" she could barely contain herself. I asked, "Which one?" "You pick," she said.

I took a look at the purple pill. I had no idea what it was but I figured it would be fun to find out so I picked it up and handed it to her. "I want purple!" She was like a puppy dog getting a treat. She washed it down with her wine. The rest of us decided to give it a few moments before we chose, waiting to see the effects on Bridgette.

About 10 minutes later, she acted like she had a hot flash and began removing her clothes saying, "It's hot in here." That was all Molly needed to see and she grabbed her purple pill. "Bridgette is ten minutes ahead of me. That's not fair," as she swallowed hers. We dubbed it the purple panty dropper. (PPD)

Angie and I followed suit and washed ours down with wine. We all felt Bridgette's warming and before long the ladies were down to their thongs and I was in my boxers. There was a bottle of baby oil in every bathroom. Buzzed, I thought how cool and collected one for each of us. Annie was first. She opened the bottle and poured it on her boobs and shoulders.

This was a signal for the 3 of us to massage Annie and smooth the oil all over her body. Annie was feeling the attention and whatever the purple pill was, accentuated the pleasurable feeling of touch from all the hands.

Molly went next and she received her full body massage. Bridgette took her turn getting really turned on from the massaging motion and finally it was my turn. The hands were everywhere. It felt great as I kept my eyes closed to better heighten the sensation.

Bridgette and Molly had moved on to their own exploration and massaging. Annie whispered, "Let's go into the bedroom honey." "Lead the way my love."

The oil on our bodies tonight made it hard to keep a rhythm going, undeterred, we grinded on. Moments later, we heard some noises down the hall. Ignoring them, we continued to make love in multiple positions. During a momentary break, we heard more noises.

We looked at each other and went to investigate. We heard crack, snap and a few more cracks and snaps. We opened the door about an inch to peek into the room. Bridgette and Molly had gone into the room with the bondage gear and toys.

With both of them sexcited after the X kicked in, Annie and I made sweet passionate love in our own room. We could no longer hear the girls down the hall.

Chapter 24

Special thanks were extended from our client. The word got out about the hit on Newman but he was able to deny it since the official cause of death was heart attack. Apparently, when he was back in his mansion, he was found dead in bed. His guards found him unresponsive. He had a huge organization and now his competitors were scrambling to control his business.

Whoever does, better not scam anyone, or at least not the wrong person. The Grinch will have our money wired into our account in a few hours along with reimbursement for the half million lost in the poker game. This is one hell of a vacation.

Today we have a full day outside on the yacht. I let them sleep in but we did unbind them about 7 a.m. Neither girl complained. It was all intense fun. I had Yodal take the bondage gear to get cleaned and disinfected. They might be needed again soon. .

We reached the dock about noon. This was practically a new 35' yacht loaded with amenities and a staff of local catalog models with boating skills. Annie was the first to be helped into the yacht. The young lad with a dark tan, curly black hair and abs to die for, wearing white shorts that practically showed his package, greeted Annie with his perfect white teeth.

Molly and Bridgette looked at each other and just smiled, licking their lips at the pretty boy as they were next to be helped on deck. I brought up the rear. I was 30, he was about 20. No way could I compete with that, yet, I'd rather be me.

As instructed the boat was stocked with Corona's, wine and champagne. We had an onboard bartender and a waitress to keep our hands filled at all times. The yacht was ours until midnight. The captain backed the yacht into higher water and accelerated forward to the waters not too far off shore.

Concern over a quick flying storm kept the captain on alert for a quick retreat if necessary. Everyone picked out a lounge chair to take in the sun with. I had the job of applying sun tan lotion on the girls but I thought they would prefer the 20 year old pretty boy so I asked him if he would do the honors.

He got permission from the captain and took care of business. Even Annie liked the way I thought. Later I had the masseuse surprise them with another relaxing massage.

It was time for some snorkeling at the Antilla Wreck, a ship built in 1929 for the Germans. Split in half just under the waters of Aruba, some of the best snorkeling I've ever experienced. We all grabbed our snorkeling gear and jumped off the yacht into the water.

It was important to control your movements because the current was extremely strong and you could be pulled far from the yacht and go into panic. That's why you sign a snorkel at your own risk waiver. The sights of the many colors and types of fish were incredible. I'd only done this about a half dozen times before and it was nothing like this.

The girls were taking it all in and all the guys were taking in the beauty of them. A win win? Finally they had enough and were exhausted and we made our way back to the yacht once again helped on deck by the pretty boy. Sorry, I don't know his name, don't care either.

Pass the Coronas Mr. Bartender. We kicked back and chilled as the sun was starting to create a beautiful sunset. No doubt, I'm retiring in the tropics. The culture is so different here. I could get used to this. We were immersed in the night air enjoying the smells and sounds of the ocean. Soon we would we be back on land and ready to extend the night.

Getting back to the room, everyone was crashing hard. We all decided to relax tonight and get a good night sleep. I told them I had another excursion planned for them to visit the island. They wanted to wait until tomorrow afternoon. I think shopping was their real plan in the morning.

I was up surprising early and went to the beach. I had left a note on the fridge where I was. A few dips in the ocean and some me time in the hammock with the sea breezes adding to the feeling of bliss I was experiencing. Finally, after several hours of me time, I went to the hotel room.

A small rain shower was sending people back and forth rather hurriedly. When I put the key in my door, a really hot young lady approached me. "Hey dude, just come from the beach?" "Sure did, it's one of God's best creations," I said. "I agree," she added. "Hey, we've got a party later tonight next door. Wanna come?"

"I have a few friends I'd have to bring," I explained. "Hey, the more the merrier, bring 'em all. I'm Lola," she said. "I'm Bill and count on the four of us to stop over," I said. "After 9 would be good, sure hope you make it," and leaned over and kissed my cheek. "Count on it Lola" and walked inside.

I found my note only to have it crossed out and they left me a note saying,"Out shopping, be back later." Cool I thought and made a roast beef sandwich from the leftovers two nights ago. I contacted Yadol and asked him to get some more of the stash he supplied me with the other night. If possible, I instructed him to double the quantity.

We just might need it for the party tonight. I turned on the news and more headlines about Newman were circulating, the news channels were debating who would be the next Newman. My job was done so I changed the channel and watched some footbol. That's not football, that's soccer. I hate that argument. Enough said.

Chapter 25

The door opened and three sexy women invaded my quiet with bags and bags of clothes, shoes, jewelry, bikinis and more stuff. We are going to have to ship this back. It'll never fit in their luggage. Well, maybe in the jet it will.

Annie did slow it down after the fashion show I gave her. Still though, at least 3 more bags. A moment later, a knock on the door and a bellman brought in a dozen more bags. Whatever, it's not my problem for now.

I informed them of a party next door at 9. You have 4 hours to relax and get your sexy butts ready. "Thanks Bill," is all I heard and everyone retreated into the bedrooms. "If anyone's hungry, there's plenty of food in the fridge." Again answering, "Thanks Bill."

I went back to watching TV, Fast and the Furious part 2. I could hear movement in the rooms and then in the showers. They were already getting ready for the night's activities. I'm sure they changed outfits at least 5 times each. I know Annie and that is her MO. I yelled out,"Pre-party at 8 ladies!" They answered as if on cue, "Thanks Bill."

I lit up a joint and inhaled deeply before exhaling. I started coughing hard. It's amazing; I hate cigarettes but love weed. A few more tokes and Molly came out for a toke or two. Then Bridgette and Annie all joined us for a couple of joints.

This was a nice mellow start to another night of partying. A knock on the door and Yadol was standing there with my stash again. I handed him a few hundred and off he went. The girls wanted to know what was in the bag. I just said, "More goodies for later."

"For us?" asked Bridgette. I nodded my head and said, "Only if you're good, or should I say bad?" I said sarcastically. I could read their expressions. I knew they were getting ready to be wild. Tonight's festivities were just getting started.

The party was starting and we were almost ready. One more check in the mirror, a handful of the purple pills and we moseyed on over. "Hello Lola," as the door opened. "And hello to you Bill," she smiled seductively at me. "These are my friends, Bridgette, Molly" "And I'm Annie," as she interrupted me. "Please come on in," grabbing my ass as I walked by.

Annie didn't see it but she had a little jealous moment during the introduction. About a dozen people were there. I was the old person there at 30 but no one looked younger than say 25. Jello shooters and a punch bowl of margaritas were at the dinner table.

All kinds of snacks and finger foods were laid out buffet style in several locations around the suite. Every time Lola would come near me, Annie would make an appearance. I loved it. Jealousy will add some spice to the night. She had me jealous not that long ago and loves making me jealous. It's payback time.

I checked with Lola to see if she minded us having a joint. She smiled and said, "Hand one over sexy." I reached in my pocket and took it out of my hand; Lola lit it taking the first toke and had me open my mouth blowing in the smoke for me to inhale. I returned the favor and Annie came over to give me the next one.

She was cool though and gave one to Lola. It was funny when Lola kissed her lips as she pulled away with the smoke. I didn't know how to react so I just watched this battle progress through the night.

Lola cranked up the music and everyone started dancing in the center of the room. There were 5 guys and 11 ladies at the party. She did say more might join us later. We drank quite a few margaritas and then started on the jello shooters. Annie put one between her legs for me to suck on. I did just that and after spitting out the tube, moved in for some additional sucking.

The next thing you know, all the ladies grabbed a jello shooter and placed them either on their boobs, or between the legs both front and back. All the guys indulged and the ladies who had their jello tube sucked clean, moved to the ladies who still had jello shooters strategically placed. It was fun until the supply of shooters was gone.

"No problem," I said. "Anyone want to try this purple pill?" "What is it?" one of the guests asked. "It makes you warm and fuzzy." My three girls quickly took one and about half the crowd joined in. I had enough for everyone.

I watched Lola as she swallowed hers. She was teasing me and pissing off Annie. About 15 minutes later, the effect of feeling hot caused everyone who took the purple pill to strip naked. Some had no undies and it made for interesting conversation. The rest saw this and joined in.

Soon we had a naked party going on. I then offered them a hit of X and in their great sexy and lfeeling mode I could have offered them hot sauce and they would have accepted. Before long, everyone was all smiles and became touchy feely.

As usual, Bridgette and Molly were in lip lock mode, caressing each other with sensual rhythms. Lola, who had that cute girl next door look going on, came over and rubbed her ass against me. I was feeling the X and so was she. We started slow dancing and I bent down to nibble on her nipples.

Annie came to my rescue and took my hand to lead me away. "Your mine baby and I'm yours. No strangers babe. Bridgette and Molly are different when we play together." "I never heard you speak like that before sweetie, I like it."

The future ground rules were set that moment. We were basically exclusive except for our little friend family. I could live with that. Lola overheard and backed off. She moved to one of the other guys despite continually looking my way. Lola wanted what she couldn't have.

An hour later, our little group gathered up our clothes. I thanked Lola for a fine party, left her a couple more joints and we parted back to our suite next door. We left naked assuming no one would be on our floor. Surprise, surprise, the extra people she thought was coming had just arrived. Wait until they open the door. Those three dudes were in for a treat.

Back in our room, Molly, Bridgette and Annie were acting suspicious. I couldn't figure it out with their current body language but I was sure I'd know soon. They walked into the other girl's room and closed the door. About 10 minutes later leaving me in the dark as to their plans put the blindfold on me and took me by the hand.

After lying on the bed, the all 3 girls joined me and aroused me with the sense of touch. Each girl had a purpose in mind but with the blindfold on, I wasn't 100% sure who was who. I tried to decipher them by their perfume but even that sensory mode was heightened.

The whole experience sent a psychological thrill I had never had before.. There's a first time for everything. I'd do it again in a heartbeat.

I smelled the aroma of a joint being smoked. They let the air out near my lips. I still couldn't see but I could smell it getting closer and finally, they gave me three shot guns in a row. I was high as a kite when they were done with me. When they let me go, I thanked them for the experience and went to my room. I was spent, high, and before another session started, declared myself done for the night.

The girls still had more energy. They partied on for at least another hour.

Chapter 26

I had the jet ready to return us all to Myrtle Beach. Before we left, we boxed all the clothes and bondage equipment and Fedexed it to our house. I would have the limo meet us and get everyone home.

I made it home just in time for my good friend, Frizzy Waters. He earned that nickname way before I knew him. His hair would get so frizzy when water or wind reached his hair. Ironically, Waters is his real last name.

He was back in town for the weekend and had his family with him. I reserved tickets to the show "Good Vibrations" at the Carolina Opry for him. I picked them up at Ocean Lakes Campground Resort about an hour before the show started. His oldest girl was aspiring to be an entertainer. Little Samantha, who wasn't so little anymore, loved shows, plays and any form of entertainment.

Frizzy, his wife and four kids couldn't wait to put their pictures on facebook and instagram. When we arrived at the Opry, I snapped their picture a multitude of times with a view of Limo behind them. The photos were posted before they hit the front door. I drove the limo to the back of the parking lot and waited there for the show to finish.

Samantha was the first to come out with several souvenirs. I had the other family members wait by the Limo and took Samantha back inside. The stage was getting closer and closer and I said, "Come on, let's goes backstage, I have someone for you to meet." As we approached, her eyes grew large watching the many performers after the show.

Cindy's room two doors away so we were close. I knocked on her door and a voice from inside said, "Come on in, doors open." "Hey Cindy, I'd like you to meet Samantha, she is an aspiring future entertainer."

They shook hands and Cindy asked, "So you want to be an entertainer." "I do, I really do." "Are you doing anything now?" Samantha smiled, "Yes, I'm in drama class, take singing and dancing lessons and hopefully I'll go to Julliard." "Wow, you have some ambition young lady, keep up the good work and never stop planning your next step."

"I will, it is so nice to meet you," said Samantha. "You too," and then they shook hands and we returned to the Limo where the rest of the family was taking pictures with strangers alongside the Limo.

I was so impressed with Samantha's enthusiasm; I made a mental note to help her get into Julliard. Clearly, she has the right attitude and direction. Everyone loaded into the Limo. We took the long way home driving by Broadway at the Beach and the Skywheel at the boardwalk on Ocean Blvd...

Finally, we made a stop for some ice cream and then back to their hotel. After a bunch of hugs with his family, they went inside and I was on my way to the office when I received a call from Nathan, the other limo driver.

His Limo broke down and had to be towed. His group of kids from the college was at Broadway and needed a 2 o'clock pickup. It was only a couple more hours until then, so I redirected to Broadway and waited on the college group.

2 o'clock was here and my phone rang. It was a very young lady on the phone who I couldn't understand with all the noise in the background. Her number was on my caller ID so I shot a text to her saying, "I'm here by the Hard Rock." She responded, "We'll be out shortly, gathering the troops now."

I started the Limo to build up the AC and waited. Soon, a very loud group came around the corner of Rodeo. Several had the tall souvenir yard beer glasses in hand as they approached the Limo.

Kate, the girl on the phone was the first to greet me. "Hi, I'm Kate, Nathan said he was sending another Limo." "Yep, unfortunately his was towed to the repair shop. I'm Bill, very nice to meet you." "Are you Limo Bill?" "That's me." "Finally I get to meet you. You are the buzz around campus. The girls think you're so hot and I agree." "Thanks."

Just then her boyfriend walks up and shakes my hand." "Hey Limo Bill, good to see you again. You took a bunch of us on my friends 21st birthday a few months ago." "Was it Darren?" I remembered him because he was so drunk and obnoxious. "Yes he said," and we both laughed remembering I nearly kicked him out of the Limo.

After they were all in the Limo, I reminded them of the $200 clean up fee after seeing a few of them very intoxicated and you just never know when something bad will happen. If anyone gets sick, let me know and I'll pull over. Please do it outside and all will be cool. I cranked up the music and began leaving Broadway. About halfway home, I approached the light at Carolina Forest and I heard a scream from the back of the Limo.

"STOP, STOP NOW!" After the light I pulled over quickly and put on my flashers. Thank goodness they told me to stop. I hate dealing with messes. I got out of the Limo to go around and check out the situation. I thought I'd see someone puking but to my surprise, two of the highly intoxicated ladies were squatted on the side and peeing out in full view of traffic from the shopping center.

Horns were blowing and guys screaming out their windows and none of it deterred them from finishing their pee. Just then a police officer pulled alongside my driver window and asked, "Everything OK?" I chuckled and said, "I've got a puker out back." He laughed saying, "I want no part of that."

If he only knew the truth of what she was really doing. These days, being arrested for peeing in public will put you on the child porn watch list for life. Hardly justified but it's the law. The cruiser sped off and the girls were once again in the Limo. It became one of those stories on campus among the many to add to the "*Just when you think you've seen it all…… category of life.*"

Chapter 27

We were approaching spring break and the hotels were gearing up for some unsavory happenings in Myrtle Beach. February was the start for a few colleges and it was spread over 8 weeks for all the colleges on the east coast. You really couldn't go in the water in Myrtle until late April but it didn't stop them from coming to the beach. Many days offered beautiful sunshine to lie out and get some tanning in. Some fools still take a dip in the ocean.

But for most, it was about the parties at night. Police had their hands full and strictly enforced the underage drinking laws. DUI's would be on the rise and the most popular shirt outside of a Myrtle Beach t-shirt was CAME ON VACATION – LEFT ON PROBATION.

It had been quiet for a while dealing with the bad guy stuff. The Grinch said be prepared for a busy year. One of his operatives was killed recently and another lay in a coma after being in the wrong place at the wrong time. I have no idea how many assassins he employs.

I do know or so I've heard the assassins have delivered 100% success over the last 4 years. I've been an assassin a little over 2 years to this point. Currently I have 27 kills, 100% bad people. I make it a point to stay focused on a job and cover all contingencies to escape from any situation. There is always another day to plan for.

I picked up a group of cute spring breakers who were visiting friends at Coastal Carolina. All the girls were from West Virginia and Ohio, all a true 10 on the 1 to 10 scale. Some left their boyfriends behind at the University of West Virginia and others were single and ready to mingle. Their second day in town, Sr. Frogs at Broadway was on the agenda. When I got the reservation to pick them up, I set my schedule accordingly.

Pulling up to the condos they were staying at, a huge roar was heard as I made my way around the parked cars and to their front door. The roar reminded me of the Heineken commercial when the screaming girls opened the closet and saw all the shoes and then down the hall another roar from the guys finding the refrigerator of beer.

Most had been drinking since noon. The 12 beauties were looking for fun and probably trouble tonight. The music was loud and they knew all the words. It was like a bad karaoke night in the back of the Limo but they were having a blast. When we reached Broadway at the Beach, they didn't want to leave; they were having so much fun.

They sang to their last song before going into Senior Frogs. At the end of the night, they returned to the Limo and were more trashed then before. That was no surprise to me. On the way back, the cameras came out, the girls kept posing for each other.

I noticed in the rear view mirror, one girl had her top off and cameras were focused on her. Then suddenly, tops were coming off and bottoms removed and they were having fun playing with each other and taking lots of pictures. I put up the divider after nearly crashing the Limo.

It was a 20 minute ride to their condos. I pulled up slowly to give them time to get dressed. When I stopped, I hesitated to open the limo door in back but it had to be done. Only 2 of the group had clothes on. The rest streaked around the Limo and then into the condos. Fortunately there were no police in view.

The last in the group gave me a big naked hug and planted a huge kiss on my cheek saying, "Thanks," as she ran off. Maybe if I was about 10 years younger and didn't have Annie, but I do and I wouldn't change it for the world.

The following morning I received a message from The Grinch. He had a new job for me and said the info would be sent by courier. That was different. Usually it was sent electronic. When the courier arrived, I signed for the package as Mr. Smith and brought it inside to check it out. There was a SD card with the information I needed. The dossier of a Hector Cortez was now in my hands after I printed it out. I destroyed the SD card as per The Grinch's instruction.

Cortez handled most of the cartels drug trade in Columbia. Authorities have worked diligently to curtail his operations but with few successes. This work order came from a secret organization inside a classified division of some government.

I don't know which government and it really doesn't matter. A job is a job and since it is paid for, it will be executed. I called Annie and asked her to come over when she had a chance. "Sure babe, see you soon," was her response.

Together we looked over the dossier for our best opportunity to get close to him. The job was marked urgent giving us just a few days to make it happen. He was in his native country now. What we were hoping for was any movement out of the country. If we couldn't find anything, the next step was to find a reason to get him on the move.

One of The Grinch's informants was contacted and working to collect any information about his exact whereabouts and upcoming schedule. The best he could confirm was a meeting with cartel leaders at the Riviera Maya in Mexico. He would be there in two days but only for dinner, meetings and back on a plane after the fire show.

That was good news to get this opening where I have been on a few vacations to. I knew the layout and had to find a way to get closer than his guards were to him. I just needed a chance to give him a handshake and inject the EOL.

Annie packed a few things for Mexico and I had the jet fueled and ready to go. We would leave in an hour to finalize our movements and where we expected to make close contact. I asked her to reach out to Bridgette and Molly if they were available for a quick vacation. The added beauty would help be a distraction.

I told her to tell them a trip to Riviera Maya and then Cancun for a couple of days. I knew they would love a getaway to warmer weather if they had the time available. Both accepted the invitation despite the very short notice.

The four of us were in the air shortly. Our flight crew was very attentive and the bar was well stocked for a private jet. Annie and the girls were chatting away while I continued to gather as much intel in preparation for tomorrow. Part of the plan was getting there early and making a scene with my gorgeous friends.

I knew Cortez would have people on the ground checking everything out in advance of his arrival. I needed to be seen as a high roller. This resort is pretty exclusive. Coming and going is from the same entrance and our resort's landscape was private. Only guests of the resort were allowed to be here.

We met many guests by the pool and ocean. Buying drinks for everyone a couple of times, I now had many friends. I invited them to the open bar area later to celebrate one of the girl's birthday. Annie played the role of birthday girl with Bridgette and Holly along for the party. We told the two of them this was to have fun with the crowd..

Nearly 100 guests showed up to party late into the night. The booze was all inclusive for guests. I ordered six dozen bottles of champagne to have a celebratory toast to the birthday girl. All the hoopla worked and Cortez knew about the birthday party. He even saw video of the three lovely ladies hanging on me and each other from his surveillance before arriving.

When he finally arrived, nearly two dozen body guards checked the grounds out first and then Cortez made his entrance. He was a short dude but had a lot of political power, especially in the drug distribution world. Over the next few hours, several of the men here for the dinner and meetings to follow, seemed to control over half of the resort's beach front. It looked like all business and that was not good news.

In between the dinner and the meetings, I conveniently positioned the four of us in view of everyone leaving the restaurant. I undoubtedly had the three hottest ladies at the resort arm in arm as we walked by

Cortez and his men. He had the guard stop us abruptly and we acted surprised all the while knowing this was part of the plan.

"Are you the pretty lady who had a birthday party last night?" She ran her finger across her lips and pulled it out to say, "Yes I am, do you like to party?" He smiled, "On occasion." "We're having round two tonight at the fire show, care to join us?" Cortez was a smart man, but the horny devil inside him couldn't resist a pretty girl's invitation.

"I just might take you up on that," and then he took her hand and gave it a gentle kiss and leaving him a farewell for now smile. The three ladies in unison said, "Bye." It sounded like angels to Cortez and to me too.

The meeting was over and a few of the men came out looking very frustrated about the discussions inside. Bottles of tequila and other liquors were brought to a secluded table overlooking the preparation for the fire show. It had fire eating entertainers, baton twirlers with fire, hula hoops with fire and finally the drums with that rhythmic beat. Boom-boom-boom and so on.

Cortez and his men walked toward us. We were sitting by the flag pole for a reason. My girls were strippers and we figured Cortez would take notice if they, shall we say, played around a little showing off their trade.

They took turns spinning and dancing around the poles. Sometimes they would put it between their legs suggestively. Cortez lost his focus as it moved to the girls. Soon they stopped and came back to sit with me.

He approached me and said, "what lovely assets you have my boy." "Thank you and I paused. "I'm sorry; I don't really know your name." "just call me General Cortez." I stood up to shake his hand, "please to meet you General, this is Annie, Bridgette and the redhead is Molly." After a firm handshake, Cortez was a gentleman going to each young lady and kissing the back of their hands.

"Would you care to join me for some tequila?" Molly moved to him and gave him a big old hug. "Let's do shots," Molly said. Cortez said something in Mexican and we took that as yes. Shots were poured all around. It went straight to the girl's heads. Molly and Bridgette were in high spirits by now.

They sat on Cortez's lab and started kissing each other. I doubt Cortez saw this coming. He leaned in for his turn and the girls obliged. They let him fondle their boobs and asses. It was becoming a big scene as everyone in the area was watching what was going on.

I don't know which dignitary stepped in but he had the men remove the girls and warned us to leave now or suffer the consequences. We took the hint to check out immediately which was our original plan as soon as the EOL drug was injected. Mission accomplished in my mind.

As I looked back I saw the drummers pouring paint on the tops of their drums and banging away sending colored paint everywhere. I had a car ordered to meet us in 15 minutes and we'd be at the front door pickup spot. I checked out at the front desk and met our ride and swiftly, we shuttled to Cancun for a couple of days.

The last few moments had me concerned, mostly because of identity but I think their issues were bigger than a bunch of partiers like us. The target had been injected and now it was just a matter of time.

Chapter28

Cancun was a perfect getaway. More warm sun and sandy beaches to explore. Spring breakers were here already but not in large crowds. I could only remember being this young not that long ago. Not that I regret getting older because my life is right where I want it to be with who I want to be with.

Annie was on the pool deck doing a little sun bathing. That was short lived when Bridgette and Molly came to collect her and off they all went shopping. Peace and quiet for me I thought until dozens of college kids invaded my personal space.

One young, lady who looked much older than 21, asked if she could buy me a drink. Taken back I said, "You buy the first, a Corona and I'll buy shots and 2 of your favorite drinks." "You're on sport," she said with a curious expression on her face.

The waiter came over with 2 Coronas each with a slice of lime. Waiter, "Wait 5 minutes and bring another Corona, 2 shots of the lady's choice and 2 more drinks of whatever the lady wants next." She asked, "How about 2 Absolute shots and 2 Absolute Vodka Red Bulls?" "I'll be back shortly," the waiter said.

"My name is Sandy." "Pleased to meet you Sandy, I'm Bill." "The girl knows how to drink." "Among other things," she mysteriously said. We struck up a nice conversation. We talked about her goals after college, college life, her parents and eventually boys.

She is a little older than many here and was on her way to a master's degree in business marketing. Sandy told me she was tired of the immature guys she dated in college and wanted to find a guy with a life worth being part of.

We discussed what she was looking for in a man, she made many references to be with a man like me. I explained you can't always judge a book by its cover, the oldest cliché in the book and it was written about guys like me.

"So what makes Bill tick?" she asked with a seductive sexy voice. I made eye contact with her, "Just call me a man of mystery and I'm not what you're looking for." In reality, I was exactly what she was looking for but I had a great life with Annie, my best friend and partner. I couldn't imagine a day without her in my life.

Sandy didn't accept the whole mystery thing. "What does that actually mean?" she asked. "I'm a little older with many secrets I could never divulge," was my response. Sandy became analytical, "Age is only a number and secrets are in every relationship. I get it, that's the mysteriousness you claim. Secrets are made to be broken."

"Yes, but in my case, people could die." "It's not like you're a murderer or thief, right?" "Like I said secrets. The other thing I must tell you is I have a wonderful woman in my life and she knows my secrets," I said laughing.

"I wasn't just talking about life, I want a fun fling. Besides, what's one more secret, Mr. Mystery Man?" "Touché my dear, I might be many things, but loyal is at the top of my list. I sure hope you can appreciate that?"

"OK, it could have been wild," as she grabbed her last drink, leaned over and kissed me hard on the lips. "If you change your mind, I'll be the drunk one with a see thru mesh outfit tonight with the hots for you." "Thanks for the warning Sandy, it was really nice meeting you." "You too sexy," she said smiling.

She was very sexy too but I didn't want to encourage her any more than she already was. Truth be told, she resembled Annie as if she was a barely younger her. Maybe a younger sister is the best way to describe how I see her. And that is very hot.

Why is it that you finally find someone you really care about and make a decision to see where it will go, multiple temptations keep happening. Now I'm horny. "Annie where are you!" I had no idea when the girls would be done with their shopping and I'm sure they had many sets of eyes watching their every move. She has her temptations too. It's going to take many sacrifices. I sure hope I don't f&^% it up.

"Honey, I'm home," as I heard the door open and the rustling of bags banging on the doorway as the girls entered. They sounded like they had an early start to the night. They bar hopped in between shopping. They spent most of the shopping time in the lingerie store. Some for work back at the club and some for personal pleasure.

I have never argued with Annie over her choices of lingerie because I always received a personal modeling show from her. I had a special cookout planned for us and had invited a bunch from the pool earlier. Local barbecue specialists took care of all the cooking and we had our own tiki bar fully stocked with top shelf liquor.

The smell of the barbecue getting fired up was the signal for all my new friends to come join us. About two dozen of my guests started arriving. Just on the other sides of resort, all the spring breakers were still partying like it was there last day on earth. They had completely taken over the pool area and were in tune with the DJ's every word and music.

He had them cheering and fist pumping. Thongs and skinny bras was the standard style of dress among this group. Guys were pulling strings faster than the girls could tie them, just showing their immaturity thinking they are being funny.

Our little party in comparison was pretty tame compared to the spring breakers for now. T-bone steaks, marinated chicken, Mahi Mahi, shrimp, seasoned burgers, hot dogs and some local veggies were all grilled to perfection by our awesome cook.

A snap of the fingers and your next drinks of choice were on the way to you. We had our own Reggae music being performed from a local band. It was loud enough to drown out the insane volume from the spring breakers party. Sandy came by for a visit and I noticed her right away. The mesh outfit took my breath away for a brief moment.

Annie saw her to and both were walking toward me. I quickly introduced them, "Annie, this Sandy who I met earlier when you were shopping." "Sandy, this is Annie, my very special friend and partner."

Sandy was about to approach me with another of her kisses but stopped in her tracks and shook hands with Annie. Whew! That was close I thought. Not that anything happened but I didn't want to have that conversation with Annie.

They both looked at each other in an inquisitive way. The resemblance was uncanny. I tell you they look like sisters only Annie had larger boobs. They weren't all natural but I was quite fond of them. We sat around and chatted for a while about her schooling and the conversation eventually led to men and partying.

I barely said a word, not that I could get a word in edgewise. I might as well been invisible except for the occasional nod of my head in agreement with whatever they said. Ya, I'm a typical guy. I care about Annie but Sandy sure looked hot and tempting. I'm in the look but don't do stage of our relationship. That's my story and I'm sticking to it.

We all decided to wander over to the spring breakers side and crash their party. They were pretty wild and getting high. Weed was lit up everywhere and kids were either jumping in and out of the pool or grinding on each other to the music with raised alcohol in their hands. Most were a long way from calling it a night.

Everyone was in such good spirits they never realized we were there. I did notice a few from our barbecue had disappeared back to their rooms and that was cool. This was our last night before going back to the states. It's been fun and a lot has happened in 72 hours. I'm ready to get back to our beach and some quiet time with Annie.

The party finally started thinning out. Bodies were everywhere; most were passed out on the lawn and lounge chairs. The resort crew was doing their best to wake them up and push them toward their rooms.

Two couples were having sex by the pool until security broke it up and warned them about sex in public and to take it inside so they left. Molly and Bridgette were teasing a few of the boys acting like they might have a chance with them, but that never happened. They joined us to go back to the room.

Sandy was pretty toasted and was sitting on some dudes lap when they were ushered away. The cleanup crew moved in with about 10 workers. They had their hands full but I was pretty sure they expected it.

Inside our suite, Annie and I grabbed one last Corona and disappeared into our bedroom. Molly and Bridgette we exhausted and retreated to theirs. A quick shower and I felt a little rejuvenated and so did Annie. We laid on our bed naked and Annie asked, "I thought Sandy was a lot like me, sexy, smart and driven." "I agree," I said.

"She could be your long lost sister," I said jokingly. "Ya, I wonder if she would enjoy sex with you like I do." "What, your something else, not going to happen." "I bet you thought about it though." "I'd be lying if I said no but there's a huge difference between thinking it and ever even beginning the process of doing it," I said.

"I want to be clear how much I believe in us and want to see where the ride takes us?" I added. "I know honey, I was just saying." I reached her lips and smacked a playful kiss on her sumptuous lips and squeezed as tight as I could.

We were pretty tired but that embrace triggered some horny feelings in both of us. I looked at her and said, "I owe you one, so don't argue and turn over." "I'll be right back," I said. I had the concierge make a visit to the shops and bring back a couple of bottles of lotion, melon cucumber, coconut and strawberry, to be exact. I said, "Close your eyes and choose a fragrance." She chose melon cucumber, my favorite. I squeezed some lotion onto her shoulders and started massaging her neck and shoulders with enough pressure to feel a deep massage. More lotion was squeezed onto her back between her shoulder blades and about her lower hips. I spent a good 10 minutes making sure to not miss a spot.

I added a few more squirts on to her ass and her legs. I moved around to position myself to move from ankles to ass for a good while. My lotioned fingers reached between her legs and I surprised her a bit.

Continuing a massaging motion, Annie started panting and I slid my body on hers and began making love to her and continued massaging parts I could reach of her body while easily sliding in and out before turning her over.

Kissing her very passionately, I added more lotion to her front side. Massaging her neck and shoulders, her luscious boobs, down her belly, legs and once again between her legs. Sliding once again on top of her body,

I gave her another passionate kiss and continued making love to her. We moved in rhythm as one and lasted as long as we could. I finally exploded inside her and her reaction was priceless. To end our playtime, I massaged her feet causing her to laugh form the occasional tickling feeling.

In the end, it was a perfect ending to our stay in Mexico. Our jet leaves early tomorrow, time for some sleep.

Chapter 29

The wheels were in the air on schedule. No word yet on Cortez. Sometimes, things are kept hush hush until the replacement is in place and its back to business as usual. Until I get confirmation, there is always concern.

If I wasn't sure I injected the drug in my target even if the band aid turns green because the process is so fast, I would have to trust I did it right and the specific delivery system won't fail. It's been perfect since we implemented EOL shortly after I became a high priced assassin. Each dose costs about $50,000 when you add all the research cost of the very unique chemical components used in EOL.

I am the only one who uses this method. My design and Dr. Rudi's expertise makes killing without collateral damage unique in the assassin world. Maybe someday I'll be in the Hitman Hall of Fame. LOL

It looks like everyone had a good night's sleep. There was lots of energy on the flight home from the girls. The flight seemed very quick and Myrtle Beach was a few minutes away. Nathan and the Limo was waiting our arrival and had pulled up onto the landing strip. He was challenged to fit all the shopping bags into the trunk but forced the last of them in.

A pair of panties had slipped out of one of the bags. Nathan picked it up and we all laughed. "Now what are you going to do know Nathan?" I asked. Embarrassed, he tossed it in the trunk just shaking his head walking toward the driver's door and preparing to drive.

Holly and Bridgette were dropped off on the way to our house. It took a while to determine who the proper bags belonged to. A little cat fight was about to brew. "That's mine bitch," Annie joked. "Ya, well these two are mine," Molly said grabbing the 2 making her total of bags.

It didn't really matter since they shared most outfits at the club. A few more moments of grabbing things, along with that loose pair of panties and they were done. "Call me later Annie," Bridgette yelled. "I will," Annie yelled back.

We received the good news after powering up the laptop. The Grinch sent us a message confirming the target had expired. As I thought, a scramble was on to redistribute power and confirms the cause of death. Our funds would soon be sent to our account. Go figure, we had to wait for government authorization.

I think I like the private clients better. They must clear The Grinch's account first who actually pays us. One more completed job to add to the resume. I sometimes wonder who the other assassins are and their mode of their end game. Maybe someday when I'm old and gray I'll find out, maybe never and I could live with that.

So what to do today? A trip to the gym makes sense. All this indulging in the party life, I definitely need to keep the endorphins kicking and avoid the possibility of adding any flab to this 30 year old body. Lately, the only exercise I've had lately is sex. Good Sex!

A great workout that's a satisfying workout I always look forward to but it's a different kind of workout. A trip to Planet Fitness is the plan. Plenty of locals practically live there and I get to catch up with many of them. It's a small town when rumors or stories start spreading around.

Being known as Limo Bill is perfect as a cover and keeps all my contacts unknowingly helpful as an assassin. I called Annie who had gone home and asked her to join me. She said to go ahead and she'll be by soon. She gets such a great workout dancing. The gym is more for show than results.

I ran into Kenny at the door and he started telling me about the beer tasting event at the House of Blues coming up. I missed last year's event. Hundreds of home brews sponsored by the local radio station and beer distributors for a fundraising cause is a great reason to be there. Plus, I get to see all my friends and Annie's friends. It makes for an interesting time and for some, some great story telling to tease those who overdo it.

I hit the various weight machines with my headphones cranking to Pandora. Hinder was playing and the high energy tunes help make time fly. The second half of my workout was 30 minutes of cardio on the elliptical machine. Annie came by to give me a kiss in her Under Armor sports bra and her long form fitting outfit covering her sexy long legs.

She was a dick magnet any time she came to the gym. It's no secret why, when you look at that body. Add that to her phenomenal smile and friendly attitude and you have perfection. Hey, she's my lady and I love to look at her. It's no secret others do to and why she's the most asked for at the GFE club.

It was time for my scheduled massage. I had decided on a 45 minute session today. I need a deep massage to sooth any stress from my mind and body. Annie was doing the step up machine and did some spinning.

We ended around the same time and needed a shower. We both headed to our own places with the plan to meet up for dinner. I set a time of 7 o'clock to pick her up. We had reservations at Travinia's and then a movie at the theater next door.

The movie was a chick flick she had wanted to see. We sat in the very back corner of the theater and out of sight of other movie goers. Sometimes she gets a little frisky in the dark and goes along for the ride. She wanted some popcorn with butter and bottled water.

I went to the concession stand loading up with popcorn, drinks and box of almond joy candy. The movie was a comedy love affair. Some jerky guy didn't have a clue on what his woman wanted and they broke up.

In the movie, she states she wants a guy who knows when to be cuddly, romantic, and helpful around the house, pick up his dirty laundry, and on and on. As a guy, the frustrating part is she is telling this to her girlfriend.

I wanted to stop the movie right there but I couldn't find the remote. LOL! I know, I'm being sarcastic. Listen up ladies, a guy is not psychic, he can't read your freakin' mind, he gets all screwed up trying to read your body language and using misinformation in his brain to try and please you.

Unless they are ADD, a guy will rarely initiate what you want on their own. "Just tell your dude what the f^&% you want from him if you ever want it to happen!" I blurted out in the theatre and everyone started laughing.

I embarrassed myself but I meant every word of it. Here's my message to the dudes. Ask her what she wants. You probably won't get a straight answer, but at times you will get a gem from her that you can work with and make happen. Good luck.

The crowd had forgotten about my outburst and focused on the movie. I had my arm around Annie and started to flirt with her. She put down the popcorn and reciprocated by sliding her hand between my legs. My movement consisted of reaching over her shoulder and resting a massaging hand on her boobs.

We took turns checking to see if any of the crowd was watching us instead of the movie. All clear... Ten minutes of this and we were getting worked up. We wanted to sneak down to the floor but it was a little sticky so we canned that idea. We started kissing and it got more passionate by the minute. A heckler from the crowd pointed to us and yelled, "Get her dude, get her."

We abruptly stopped, stood up and gave the crowd a bow, and then a round of cheers came from the crowd. We couldn't help notice couples chatting amongst themselves and I'm quite sure it was about us, an older couple flipped us the bird. From that point on we were good movie watchers and watched the end of the film finishing our popcorn, candy and drinks.

A friend of ours had a gig as a DJ around the corner at Nacho Hippo. We stopped there for a few drinks and some fun conversations with some people we knew. Annie was engaged in a fun discussion with a few ladies she had just met. When I walked over to her and joined in, she introduced me as her best friend.

One of the girls asked, "Are you two together 'cause you make a cute couple." Annie cut her short after seeing her man hungry eyes, "Yes we are." The whole tone had changed at that moment. "Honey, one more drink or are you ready to go?" I asked.

"Let me finish this and I'll come get you." "Cool," as I walked back to my DJ friend. I hugged her and his girlfriend telling them we were leaving. Annie was right behind me and gave a round of hugs and we headed home.

Back at the house, Annie grabbed a bottle of wine and a couple of glasses. We stripped down naked and sat in the hot tub. The next two days we both had to work our cover jobs. Some hot tub time was well deserved private time.

She sat on my lap sipping her wine and leaning her head back onto my shoulder. I sipped my wine and took in the relaxation moment we were sharing. It was so nice but sitting in the hot tub this long. I could be shriveled up like a prune before getting out but who cares.

"Damn, my phone just sounded," that sure kills the mood. "Go answer it, we know who it is and it's important," Annie said. I stepped out of the hot tub and into the kitchen where my phone was charging. Sure enough,

Chapter 30

The Grinch was letting me know he had a new client and the dossier would be sent to my laptop. I powered up the laptop and reviewed the information sent. Annie came up behind me still very naked and wrapped her arms around me looking over my shoulder at the computer screen.

A photo of the mark was on the left side and in big red letters it blinked "Very Dangerous!" "Proceed with Extreme Caution!" This was a rare message to see. To the right of his photo, the name was Adam Gertz. He goes by the name ICE in his circles.

Reading further, the dossier states he is a former navy seal and has killed several hundred on his many missions in the military and as a high profile mercenary. His reach is deep in support and has no know weaknesses among his contacts.

We had one week to complete the job and the payout was tripled. He was an ally to a particular dictator and the word is he has been commissioned to cause a major war in a neighboring country. Intel says if this happens, it could domino and change the balance of power in parts of Europe.

The U.S., Canada, Japan, China, Russia are a few countries who are concerned. I don't get it because of the geography of where this list of countries is located and it doesn't directly line up as a domino, but I'm not a military strategist.

This is one of the more detailed dossiers I've seen. If there was a weakness, it was probably his family living here in the states somewhere in Texas. His parents were still alive but his mom was in and out of the hospital for cancer treatments.

She was getting top of the line care medically and given an experimental cancer killing drug which hasn't eliminated the cancer but has slowed the process dramatically. Word is, the doctors give her up to a year as long as the experimental drug doesn't have bad side effect her body can't handle.

"I'm not sure if I'm the right person for this particular job," I told Annie. "The one rule I have is no collateral damage. For that reason I don't want to involve family." She responded, "I know what you are saying. Let's do some research and see what we find."

"We will," I said and looked back at the files for a way to reach him. One week might not be enough time making this job impossible. An important factor to keep in mind is not being connected to this in the end.

I studied the files time and time again, as if we read each other's mind, we said it simultaneously. "Get ICE to come home for his mom!" It's the only way thing makes sense. He should be careful about the size and noticeable appearance of his entourage around his parents along with setting off red flags entering the country.

He's a top target for Interpol, just one of many agencies who monitor his movements as much as possible. He is a master at the shell game and diversion tactics. We found his weakness, now we have to create a fool proof plan getting close to him.

The next day, Annie and I once again reviewed the parents information. A satellite photo showed they lived in a small neighborhood and there was some property up for sale. I had a friend who lived in San Antonio, just 25 miles outside the property where ICE's mom and dad lived. We flew out to Dallas.

I had to contact my Limo customers for the night. Nathan was available so I had him contact the spring breakers and make all he necessary arrangements for the evening. Annie cancelled at the club for the night disappointing several or her regulars. Too bad for them.

We would go as a young professional couple whose company, Addison Paper Supply, one of many fictitious companies we had built websites for appearing to be legitimate businesses from the New York and New Jersey areas. We were listed as a broker for supplying paper in all forms such as copier paper, forms, and janitorial uses and so on.

For some reason, you tell people you're a business from those states and most people not from there give it instant credibility. We contacted our telephone service to answer 800 calls or even local forwarded calls. If he does a quick check, it sounds legit and buys us some time.

We made appointments with the local real estate broker handling the property. After seeing the property and its relative closeness, I paid for it with paperwork showing it as a corporate purchase for management relocating use or a rental property. It was still furnished so we gave them a fair offer for it. The sellers were thrilled and we had our in.

The neighbors were good old country folk. Most had lived in Texas all their lives and the rest were long time Texans form nearby cities. I had instructed for the real estate company to remove the for sale sign immediately. Stop all advertising and remove the property from the MLS.

I used the excuse that our company wants to keep this in house and in my situation, other executives are not to know how the company paid for it, so please keep this transaction in confidence. I told them I know how realtors talk but to please not discuss our arrangements.

I'll be back in two days to sign all the documents with our corporate attorney.

It's a public record which makes it hard to completely hide but it would take until after we moved in before it would be noticed. By then, I hope the job is complete we'll make it a rental property managed by the real estate company that handled the transaction.

We flew back and spent some alone time watching an old movie, enjoying some wine and called it a night early if you call early 2 a.m. I was a little on edge with this particular job. We had a plan which still had some moving parts to shore up.

The next big step was getting word to ICE that his mom was in very bad shape and needed extra care with her cancer. In the meantime we needed to sit tight and let the realtors do their job and get a local attorney for the paperwork.

Chapter 31

The following night, Annie and I both made it to work. Instead of another spring breaker group, I had a mixed bachelor and bachelorette party. Seven couples from near Raleigh North Carolina. 90% of the time it's dudes or dudettes as a pre wedding group. This was one of those ten percent times. They were all family of various ages. The bridesmaids were sisters and sister-in-laws. Same deal for the groomsmen, brothers or brothers-in-law.

The ladies had dressed up in black dresses and wore their sashes saying bridesmaids and the bride to be wore a white veil. The men looked like they just got off work. They all wore jeans and plaid shirts. Most of the ladies smoked causing a delay in getting started so they could finish their cigarettes.

The guys who chewed and I think it was all of them, carried their bottles to spit in as they entered the limo. Some very elaborate tattoos were displayed on their arms and necks of both the bride and groom's side. When they spoke, the southern twang left no mistaking them for a Yankee.

Jesse and Jolene, the future bride and groom were having a little spat about one of the wives who always tried to run things. She was not the maid of honor and no one elected her queen bee for this night. It took me about 2 minutes to determine who the bitch was using the bride to be's words. Everyone was drinking for many hours before I picked them up.

Cassidy, the bitch's name, was talking very loudly and seemed to be complaining about who knows what and who really cares attitude came from the body language of the rest of the party including her husband. Cassidy was probably 23 or 24 best guess. I turned up the club mix music loud enough to get them in a party mode and not in an argumentative state of mind.

It worked as the Limo was rockin' from the jumping around antics of several guys and gals in the Limo. We took the trip from Ocean Lakes going north on ocean boulevard past the Skywheel and then turning on 21 avenue north to Broadway at the Beach.

Rodeo had the Josh Brannon Band playing until 10 p.m. tonight playing their favorite country music and many of the songs from their latest CD. Of course Jesse and the big mouth Cassidy had to ride the bull at Rodeo.

I swear the person controlling the bull's movement was hard on the guys sending them flying off in a very short ride. One of the bridesmaids slipped a ten spot to send Cassidy on the mat in less than 5 seconds. She got what she paid for and captured it on video. Ten bucks well spent.

It went viral on facebook within minutes. "Nice one," I told her. She smiled and said, "I like you Mr. Bill." I said a quick hello to Josh and the band and went back to the Limo to move it around the corner and out of the way of incoming group drop offs.

When the band was done, Jesse called me saying they were ready. A little drunker and louder, they came back to the Limo. I was hugged 4 times as they all made it into the Limo. "Strip club!" they yelled. Tonight was Saturday and the male revue was open for the ladies.

The guys went in the main entrance to the Gentleman's Club. I was rented until 1 a.m. so I reminded them they need to be out by 12:30. I opened the driver's door and sat down grabbing my laptop to do some research for the important job ahead of us.

A message from The Grinch said he had arranged for a lawyer to be at the realtors office along with the sellers around 4 p.m. their time. Annie and I had planned on leaving by 10 a.m. to make sure we wouldn't be late in case of any delays. If there were, we'd have time to adjust our plans.

At 12:15 I stopped into both clubs to find my now out of control groups. They had kicked two of the ladies out about a half an hour ago for inappropriate behavior and they went to the men's side. They were in a male revue club. What's inappropriate behavior? Never mind, I don't want to know.

The rest of the girls were getting chair dances with dicks in their faces and sweat dripping on them from the dancers. Most of them couldn't care less. These women were insane. And then I understood what inappropriate behavior was. One lady tried to suck a dancer's cock. That person was removed from the building but the person in trouble this time was part of a different group.

Over at the other club, three were in the back room getting a private dance. When the next song ended, I located all three and we walked to the rest of the group and forced a group exit. We now had the full crew in the Limo. The stories were flying around the back.

It was easy to tell who didn't want to be in a strip club. They had no stories. Actually, they didn't say a word all the way home. They just stared at their significant other trying to make them feel guilty. That's a conversation I want no part of. I changed it to the country channel and turned up the volume. It seemed to help calm the upset ones down.

Pulling the Limo to the front of their places is always a challenge with Ocean Lakes' small streets and corners. Golf carts are flying every which way and many without any lighting on the dark streets. They'd be history if the Hummer Limo ran them over. I had to be extra cautionary. I might be an assassin but running someone over is not my MO, yet.

Several hugs and handshakes later, Jessie, Jolene and their group of rednecks were home safe and sound. I could still here the bickering going on with Cassidy and her husband. Everyone else avoided them like the plague.

It always amazes me how many times someone in a group makes the night about them, specifically Cassidy types, and puts a damper on the fun for who the party is intended. Drama queens come in the forms of both the ladies and the guys. Never assume anything is the rule.

Sometimes it's their hair, the clothing, something someone said or an attitude that sets them off. I say, "Shut up and bud out." If you're not supporting your friend, step into the background. And you know who you are.....

Chapter 32

Now that we have the lawyer in place, we need to get ICE to his mom's house. We flew back to the new house and made an appearance before going to the real estate office and complete all the paperwork. Addison Paper Supply now owned a property Annie and I would take residence in for now.

Our first order of business was to meet ICE's parents. We designed a hello card to pass to all the neighbors. Introducing ourselves as Tom and Samantha Griffin, no children yet and I was transferred in by Addison Paper Supply and Samantha was my office manager/wife and we moved here to grow a new territory in the Southwest U.S. She used a ring from Aruba's fashion show we bought.

We were dressed like we were going to a dinner meeting. Now it was Showtime. We knocked on every door in the neighborhood and introduced ourselves as their new neighbors. Gave them our hello card and told them we looked forward to seeing them around. There were about 40 homes in the neighborhood. We saved the Gertz's residence (ICE's parents) for last.

Mrs. Gertz answered the door. Immediately you could tell she was sick. "Hello neighbor, we are your new neighbors. I'm Tom and this is Samantha." "Hi, I didn't know we had new neighbors," said Mrs. Getz. "Our company bought the Zimmerman's house, nice couple," I said. "Yes they are, we hated to see them move but they wanted to move closer to their grandchildren," she responded.

Kids are a whole other scenario for Annie and I to contemplate I thought. "I understand that, they were looking forward to it so much when we signed the papers," I added. "Can I interest you in tea or coffee or a beer" I looked at Samantha and she nodded yes, "Coffee sounds great." "Come, sit down and relax. Frank, come meet our new neighbors."

"I'm sorry, I didn't get your wife's name," I said to Frank. "It's Marie." The four of us acted as if we knew each other for years. They gave us a lay of the land and some history on the neighborhood. The conversation came up about kids and we said none yet but maybe soon.

They had a son and two daughters, Adam, Ann Marie and Becky. They thought Adam was still in the military. If they found out about Adam, they would be shocked into a heart attack knowing the truth about their son. Ann Marie and Becky lived within 100 miles from here, a school teacher and hair stylist.

Annie asked, "Marie, I couldn't help but notice you look a little weak." "Its cancer, they tell me I don't have long," she quietly said. "I'm so sorry, I didn't mean to pry." "It's OK, I outlived previous predictions and I ain't dead yet," as she laughed a bit and then a hacking cough. "My dad has cancer too. He beat it once but we're braced for that scary call," Annie said.

"I try not to think about it, it's the hospital visits I hate," Marie said. How could such nice couple like Frank and Marie have such a bad son, killing so many to get where he is.

I was looking around at the pictures of ICE in his military uniform and their lovely daughters. I felt sorry for them and I knew I had to take care of business with so many lives at stake, but if it was possible, I wanted to at least let them remember the goodness in their son.

I sent a message to The Grinch that I needed help in getting a message to ICE that it was urgent he go see his mom. Say the cancer has spread and her time to live was an issue. Somehow, she had mentioned she wishes to have her son make a surprise visit. I'm not sure what the actual message was but it worked. I do know he faked hospital records.

The Grinch used undercover agents to reach out to ICE. He was returning to the states under an alias to avoid detection. If he was captured along the way that would avert the danger and my services were no longer needed. All we knew is he would reach his parents tomorrow evening.

We invited the whole neighborhood for a cookout for the next evening. It was imperative the Gertz's were among the group. We had it catered to allow us to mingle among the crowd and not miss our opportunity. The turnout was a success.

75% of the neighborhood came to visit and have, burgers, chicken, hot dogs and more. Some of the neighbors brought desert and side dished like home recipe baked beans, fiery chili and barbeque. It was a feast and a lot of fun. We met some neighbors our age and some of the kids in the neighborhood.

Finally the big moment arrived. Frank and Marie came down the street on her motor scooter. Her face was lit up with the thrill of getting outside and seeing everyone again. Everyone stays inside so much, many neighbors only see each other when they are coming and going. Aimee fixed them a plate and some sweet tea.

It was about an hour later ICE showed up in a rental car. I quickly prepared the EOL for injection. We stayed near Frank and Marie as soon as we saw him step out of his car. He made a straight bee line to his mom and gave her a giant hug. This guy was huge, muscular huge. I didn't see that in the pictures.

I asked him, "Would you care for a burger and something to drink?" "I'm starving so sure," he said. "Annie chimed in, "What would you like? Beer, Sweet tea, Hamburger, Hot Dog?" she asked. "Hamburger and a beer would do it." He and his mom and dad were having a family moment. Mom was thrilled and surprised.

Annie came back with his burger and beer. "Here you go." "Thanks." Marie then introduced us, "Have you met Tom and Samantha?" "No I haven't." "Adam, this is Samantha and Tom the host for this cookout." Annie shook his hand, and then I did the same with a firm handshake.

I moved away and let Annie charm him for a bit. I took the focus off me and had brief conversations with several of our guests. About 30 minutes later, Annie and the Gertz's were still having a conversation. Annie was a pro at conversation from her experiences in the strip club. By now the party was winding down.

We all said our goodbyes over time and we found ourselves alone in the house. We needed to stay here until ICE left. It was important to keep up our cover image until then. A trip to the grocery store to stock the fridge was a great cover.

We saw Brad and Emma out by their truck and asked them for directions to the nearest grocery store. Then I asked them to join us and show us around. Our two new friends jumped in and took us to Wal-Mart. Go figure.

A few bags of non perishables would do it and it also worked well for cover. Being seen with neighbors and buying groceries was a natural thing people do when they want to appear they live in a neighborhood. We knew ICE wouldn't be here long and we sure didn't want him snooping into our background. The next day, I cut the grass and I had a box truck deliver an office desk to continue our cover.

I hadn't figured out how to get out of here yet short of disappearing. ICE was outside looking over the neighborhood for anything suspicious. Several of the neighbors were outside and I stopped from mowing long enough waving hello and he waved back. I continued mowing and he went back inside.

When we were shopping with Brad and Emma, we asked about the condition of Marie. They felt for the family as if they were family. The Gertz's lived her for 40 years and are original owners in the neighborhood. We decided to make a friendly visit with a few other neighbors, then to her house and wish her the best on her visit to the hospital tomorrow.

It would show our concern and make the urgency for him visiting his mom more justified. We gathered together at Brad's house and walked over to wish the family the best. We didn't stay. We just wanted to show we cared. Annie and I really did care about Marie. She was a trooper and it was easy to see she had a heart of gold and why people cared about her. I can't say the same for her son.

The buzz around the neighborhood was Marie was responding to her treatments. Part of the process was the few bad days they had seen her suffer with. Now, with the improvement in Marie, ICE was leaving soon.

The concern now was when the 24 timer sounded and the EOL would have completed the job. I didn't want it to happen here, being near his mom. With about 5 hours to go, he was on his way to the airport. The EOL caused heart attack kicked in while he was waiting on his connecting flight.

Because of his alias passport, his real name was never mentioned on the news. The Grinch had operatives in place to follow him and removed his body in a secure duplicate looking ambulance. The US secret service handled all the necessary arrangement of his autopsy and identify verification and to not alarm the parents of this covert operation and ICE's death.

The parents weren't aware of anything. It was life as usual for them. The plan would be to notify them sometime in the future, maybe. A government award for losing his life in duty for his country. The truth would never be told to anyone.

Chapter 33

Some of my favorite college groups had big plans for a Friday night out. There were three birthday's being celebrated. Two turned 21 at midnight and the other turned 21 two nights ago. The pickup was at 10:30 and 2:30 a.m. Pulling into the party zone with the Hummer brought curiosity and plenty of shouts.

Some were in different college parties. My group headed by Bailey had nearly 60 kids covering over four garage doors that were open. Everyone was milling back and forth between the four houses. The police had already been by checking on the noise and checking for underage drinking. They were warned to lower the volume.

These partiers have been through this before and had plans in place to avoid any arrests. Bailey and her boyfriend came right out when I pulled up. I had the music down low because I've been reprimanded before when I came in with the music blaring through the neighborhood. Bailey said they would be ready in a moment as soon as they collected all the money.

"Remember, only 14 total Bailey," as she walked away. She turned around and pointed at me,"I know." A group of students came out at once. I asked who the birthday kids were and 3 hands went up in the air. Two of the blond girls needed some help just getting to the Limo, let alone getting in.

I did a head count and the number was exactly 14, my limit. Red solo cups were in everyone's hands. I never saw any liquor but I was sure they were refilling the cups during the 30 minute ride to Bubba's in Murrells Inlet and then to the Hot Fish Club.

The birthday girl in red was very intoxicated. When midnight hit and she was officially 21, her whole attitude changed. She acted empowered to make a fool of herself. There was a live band playing on stage and Aimee for some unknown reason went up on the stage.

She knew the words to the song and stumbled across the stage to join in. Banging her head on the lead singer didn't deter her for even a second. In a drunken way off key voice, she tried singing into his mic at the same time as the lead singer. She was dressed in a red low cut short skirt, black stiletto boots and her very blond hair did catch the eye of the band.

Little did they know what they were in for? They tried to get her off the stage while continuing on with the song. The bouncers came from the front door checking ID's to assist the managers request to remove her from the stage.

Seeing them getting on stage, she grabbed the mic and yelled, it's my 21st birthday and sat her ass on the stage. Her short skirt did little to hide the fact she had no panties on underneath. Fingers were pointing and the crowd was in awe shouting approval at the sight of her antics.

Aimee further embarrassed herself when they tried to pick her up and a boob popped out. Cameras were in picture and video mode to help remember this special birthday. It went viral in minutes and she got a call from her sister reprimanding her for her actions.

Bailey was drunk and in the moment. She was clueless until she saw all the videos later. It was a 21st birthday to remember, or not. I was in the crowd watching the events. It all happened so fast, no one saw it coming.

Even my generation 10 years ago did a lot of memorable and idiotic things. It seems like this generation, anything goes. Life rules don't seem to apply. Maybe it's just that I'm a little older. I think about how these zany activities will affect their future job opportunities when employers do their background checks and skeletons in their closet pop up when it matters. Oh well, I have my own skeletons to deal with.

With everyone watching Bailey including her boyfriend, the other two birthday celebrations went under the radar. Both were drunk and already in hangover mode. I'm sure they've been drinking hours before I arrived to gather them up and start the night with me. Now it was time to get them out of the Hot Fish Club and get back to Fairways to avoid a late charge.

As soon as I mentioned late charge, they put their asses in gear and we found all but 1. No luck trying to reach them by phone or text. She knew the schedule that was set. I said she had 5 more minute, s minus the 40 seconds that had passed and we began heading to where it the night started.

It was a 30 minute ride and one of the kids plugged in their phone to the auxiliary cord from the stereo. They played DJ and chose some funky music I never heard before. It was part reggae and part hip hop. They loved it and were moving to the music. All the lights were turned down so all I could see was shadows in the back of the Limo. Soon I noticed arms in the air and tops coming off.

Whatever their motivation, they were being naughty. Bodies were blending together and at that point they put up the divider for the remaining 15 minutes. Of course my mind was racing to determine exactly what was going on. I'd know soon enough. I had to slow down to enter the neighborhood. That was their signal I was almost home.

One wise guy in the back took all the shirts and threw them out the window just before stopping. I didn't see him do it but I heard a lot of yelling and cussing at somebody, when I walked back to open the door letting them out, 12 of them came running out with no shirts on and two girls had no pants on, just panties. It was like a fire drill and they were running for their lives.

The only dude dressed was the one who tossed the tops as a prank. He was made to go and retrieve the clothing in the street. I did find a pair of panties and three bras during cleanup.   I never expected it from this group.

Chapter 34

Annie had an easy night at work last night. One of her rich regulars (John) had his girlfriend experience with her. They spent the night chatting and he kept her supplied with alcohol and she kept him supplied with hugs and smiles. That's all this dude ever wants.

Good old undivided attention. He's about 60, a good looking guy with short white hair. Always dresses in a nice pair of slacks and a dress shirt but no tie. I've met him a few times checking up on my groups at the club.

Our account was updated while we were partying. The Grinch notified me by phone message and the rather large payout of $2.2 million was secured in our off the radar account. Lately, the payouts have been larger than normal due to specialized jobs, their timing and unique danger to so many people. The great news is our reputation has grown in certain channels.

Tonight was our night to go to a private party at the House of Blues. My friend Allan invited us. It was an anniversary party for one of the clubs in town. The owner wanted to treat his employees and friends to a private party and get them away from the club. They shut down for the night and splurged for this party. I knew Red the owner and he's used my Limo services before. Always the professional in everything he puts his name to.

This party had an extra reason to do some celebrating. Annie and had mingled among our friends while learning of our reward. "How about two Vodka Red Bulls?" I asked the bartender. I paid him and went to find Annie.

I noticed my sweet Annie getting all the attention at the table across the room. The band members from the concert next door came to crash our party and landed at the table where the most beautiful girl in the room was.

The rock band was a tribute band to an 80's group. With their leather jackets and makeup, it was clear they were Kiss wanna be's. Personally, I love Kiss and a good band, which this tribute band was by reputation can bring the many who's seen the original band, some special memories more pronounced than just on a record, cassette or CD. :

Listening to a live band versus a CD is like watching a movie in a theater versus a DVD on your TV no matter how great your sound system is.

I was driving so my drinks were cut. A DUI would not be good. It could possibly bring up things in a background check I certainly do not want to deal with. It could even affect my assassin business, particularly because I'm not ready to retire yet.

I caught Annie's attention and moved in her direction. A few hellos along the way and I wrapped my arm around her giving her a gentle kiss on her cheek.

We made our rounds saying goodbye to all and a big thank you to our host for inviting us and having such a good time. Seeing all the attention Annie was getting charged me up a bunch. It was relatively early when we left. "I can't wait to get into the hot tub." Annie said. "I second that thought." It was a 20 minute ride home.

The radio had great music on tonight and we sang the words as best we could. She knew them better than me. I lost the words way too often but I didn't care. We made it home and dressed down for some hot tub pleasure.

We put our curtain around the deck to block the view of the hot tub because the beach had many walkers enjoying the ocean breezes with their feet in the sand. Once in the hot tub, I removed my boxers and Annie her bra and panties. She climbed on my lap and we started making out very passionately with lots of tongue.

Massaging her ass and back kept my hands busy. Annie massaged my back while in a deep embrace. The effect of our bodies touching, the kissing, our hands massaging each other and the flowing jets combined with the alcohol really heated up our sensations.

After about 15 minutes of this, Annie led me into the bedroom still soaking wet. We didn't care about drying off. Lying on my back, she worked her lips down my body. I was all revved up.

She was building up a climax from her moans and gyrations. I found her G Spot and zeroed in my affection. Her body language told me I hit the target. She gyrated so hard from the sensation.

Squeezing her ass harder and playing with her G Spot put her over the edge. A magical moment we aim for every time but never hit enough.

It's like a real pot of gold at the end of a rainbow. Satisfying my woman satisfies me even more than me being satisfied. I don't know if that makes me selfish depending on how you look at it, but it's not always about me.

After our sensual and explosive love making, we curled up on the couch together and watched a movie eating ice cream and popcorn. We used our laptops to check our emails and facebook accounts before turning them off and lights down low. I wrapped my arm around her shoulder and held her tight.

She looked at me with a smile and turned back to the watching the movie. It was the Ugly Truth playing once again. We both liked comedies and good reruns never got old. I wanted to see that dinner seen and the remote control panties. I think I'll pack the remote control next trip.

Chapter 35

Today, I have an early gig. One of my previous bachelorette groups is back in town. This time is for the wedding. Katy and Kevin are doing a beach wedding at the Myrtle Beach State Park by the pier. It was hot but windy making it a bad hair day and a tough picture day. I talked with the maid of honor to finalize the plans and make time for them to add Just Married on the Limo windows.

I explained to Alicia, the bridesmaid, air conditioning is at a premium on 90 degree plus days. Too many people in the Limo add to the heat inside. They narrowed it down to ten which in dress clothes and gowns fills up the Limo quickly. There hotel was about 15 minutes from the State Park.

I remembered them when they came out of the hotel. They looked gorgeous in their gowns. All the ladies were fussing over Katy and the lady photographer was taking photos that started in the room and all the way to kissing inside the Limo.

All the groomsmen and the groom were at the park already. Kevin couldn't stop sweating and just wanted all the fuss to end. He had planned the honeymoon offered by a friend whose house was in Sunset Beach, North Carolina. The countdown was 2 hours and ten minutes until his life changed forever. He was in love and being 21 had not really experienced much of adult life.

Katy told me in conversation when I last met her at the bachelorette party, he still plays video games, goes out with the guys too often, among a few other things that bothered her. He does have a good job working for his dad's business.

I asked her if she was ready for this and having Kevin as a husband. She had her doubts but said what the hell, I love him. God bless her. The one thing I chuckled at was a reference to changing him. That's a conversation above my Limo stories grade. I knew they needed to learn that on their own for better or for worse.

The big moment was here. We arrived at the pier and Alicia was pushing everyone into place before the bride to be was to get out. The photographer was doing her job snapping pictures by the dozens. She was so beautiful in her wedding dress. The best man signaled all the men to meet on the beach.

A canopy was in place over the white carpeting laid out on the sand. Flowers were along the posts of the canopy. Reverend Dave was clutching his bible with bookmarks in place. Kevin and Katy had written their own vows.

The waves sounded in the background with the sea breeze causing those at the beach for the service shielding their faces from the blowing sand. A video camera was perched on a tripod to record this blessed day. Visitors in town were watching down from the pier snapping pictures from phones and cameras. Everyone on the beach was bare foot except the Reverend.

A rather large boom box was queued up and started playing the traditional wedding song entrance. Katy's dad led her to Kevin standing by his best friend, the best man. The Reverend was smiling as he watched Katy coming toward him. Dad gave his daughter a kiss when they reached the Reverend Dave and walked over to the side.

Powerful words were spoken by the reverend about honoring each other, for better or for worse, 'til death do us part and other words of importance. Kevin and Katy spoke their vows to each other and the blessed rings were placed on each other's fingers. A big kiss and a wave to the family and friends in the crowd and now they were officially married, paperwork and all.

While the ceremony was taking place, Alicia had a family member write on the Limo's windows the words; Congratulations, Just Maried, Katy and Kevin, Time for the Honeymoon to begin. I laughed because they spelled married wrong. The photographer took about a hundred beach photos of the whole bridal group fighting the wind and sand.

Shortly afterward, we reloaded with just the newlyweds in the Limo and to their resort. The Landmark is where the reception was to take place. About 70 guests were expected at the reception.

I put up the divider to give them some smooching piracy and reminding them we'd be there in 15 minutes. When we arrived out front, I opened the door to let them out. I moved slowly to give them time to regroup. One never knows what is going on in back with the divider up.

I didn't look in at first not to embarrass them, just in case. She was adjusting her breasts and he fixing his hair. The photographer was there to capture the newlyweds leaving the Limo. I gave both of them a hug wishing a great honeymoon and a terrific marriage. They thanked me for being part of their special day. My day was done.

Now that these two were married, I reflected on Annie and me. We weren't married but sitting with her last night on the couch like a real couple, sent my mind wondering if we could do the marriage thing. For now, we love our time together and our lives as they are. Still, I can't help think of Annie often and wonder.

Chapter 36

The Grinch needed our services. A new dossier was sent while I was working the wedding. Elvis Joseph Conner had been a bad boy. The dossier shows Conner is a serial killer preying on wives of Smart Life Technologies executives.

The information shows Conner's wife worked for the company about a year ago. She was caught cheating with Mr. Thompson, the CEO and was given a severance package to make the situation go away. It all seemed fine until Elvis found a memo slip in one of her folders.

He had his suspicions as to why she was let go. Elvis was a loser and his wife Beverly was the income of the couple. The finances crumbled after being fired and she filed for divorce. Elvis blamed her company for all the bad happening in his life, never owning up to his faults.

The police were baffled putting these scenarios together. Three spouses of executives were killed from bazaar carjackings. Two women and one man were killed. Elvis was getting bold and warned the CFO screwing his wife. Thompson's wife was next, blackmailing them to pay him 2 million dollars and the killing would be stopped.

In the note, he pointed out Mr. Thompson, the CEO had cheated with his wife and it's the reason his wife was fired and now we lost everything. You have 48 hours to comply or your wife dies and he'll take it to the TV reporters.

An emergency board meeting was called to discuss the situation. It was agreed, getting the police involved would only bring bad press to this. They would have paid the ransom demand if they didn't know Elvis was responsible for the three spouses and the new threat. The knowledge of the killer gave them a target and that was our job to end further killing.

A phone call was made and that ransom money would be paid to our firm as redemption for the death of Elvis and to eliminate any further threats.

Bottom line, I had a job to do and Elvis was my target. He was a victim too but his retribution was a bad choice. He did live near Charleston, South Carolina which is near us. The photo in the dossier and his hangout locations listed gave us enough information to locate him. His most common place to hangout was a local bar just around the corner from his apartment.

A trip to make a visual contact was in order. Annie put on some tight jeans and a revealing top. If she couldn't get his attention, no one could. The hour and a half drive went by pretty quick. With help from Google Maps, we found his neighborhood. We located the bar around the corner. It was a dive bar for locals as the dossier said.

We stopped into the bar and didn't see him. Annie was a hit though with several dudes ready to kick my ass if she wanted them too. I tried to strike a conversation but it was useless at first. Annie picked up a pool stick and smacked a few balls into the pocket. She was a vision every time she bent over the table and her boobs nearly fell out. She became the starting point for some conversation.

I overheard one of the dudes mention Elvis' name. I couldn't quite make out what they were talking about. Something wasn't right. The discussion continued about Elvis, but it was still too low for the rest of us to hear. I didn't want to cause a red flag. I walked over to Annie and said, "Let's go honey, our dinner reservations are almost ready." We left with everyone watching Annie's ass swaying back and forth.

A message came to my phone about 10 manures later letting me know Elvis was on the move. Details to come shortly and to stay put. Elvis had a plan. He wanted to put pressure on the CFO to pay up by going to his home and starting a fire. It was just a message but received very clearly. The details were sent to me. Tonight had to be the night. He's now unpredictable.

We watched the entrance of the bar and stayed real close. An hour later and we finally saw Elvis. Annie knew what to do from here. She approached the bar to meet him about the same time Elvis would be within a few feet of the door. Annie, in her high heels purposely caught her heel in the crack of the sidewalk and fell to the ground.

He couldn't resist helping a beautiful woman who had one boob showing and pushing it back into her shirt; "You OK?" rushing to her aid. She said, "I think so, I hate when this happens." It all happened so fast and before he knew it, I came around the corner. "Honey, are you OK?"

"I think so; the nice gentleman helped me up." "Thank you man, we really appreciate it," I said putting my hand out for a handshake. He reached his hand out and I gave him a firm handshake to make sure the EOL drug was injected.

Annie steadied herself with a limp from the broken shoe. Smiling she said, "Thank you so much, I'm Candy." "I'm Elvis, you're welcome." I joined in, "I'm Bob thanks again. Annie leaned over and gave Elvis a hug and a smile. He was smitten.

We avoided going in and left the area immediately. When this blows up in the news, it will never be associated with us as even being in the bar. The focus should be on the deeds he did.

We notified The Grinch we made contact with Elvis Conner and in 24 hours he will be terminated. I also told him to reach out to the CFO and his family. They needed to be out of town someplace safe. He agreed and took care of it. 24 hours might be too late for the CFO since it will be beyond the deadline Elvis set. No point in taking chances with a serial killer.

I dropped off Annie at her place. She had Bridgette coming over for a little girl time. I didn't mind. I had a few calls to make and shore up plans for an upcoming party I was planning. I didn't have any theme or reason, I just wanted to throw a barbecue and invite some friends.

Chapter 37

I got a call from the realtor in Texas about our property. He just wanted to ask me when I would be in town next. He had my paperwork finalized and my copy was ready. I told him I'd get back to him. Maybe a getaway for Annie and I would be nice and I could make some decisions about the property.

So far, everything was cool with our job. No news yet about Elvis. His time would end by this evening. The only concern was what happens when Elvis' deadline passes; I decided a swim in the pool would be good and then a hot tub massage. Looking out over the deck, I could see a couple having sex a few doors down by the fence. It was getting dark but you could still see them.

I put a ballgame on, grabbed a beer watching it from the hot tub. I could hear the phone ringing in the kitchen. It was Annie giving me a quick call. "Turn to channel 15." It was a Breaking News showing a major fire in Charleston.

The home of the CFO was blazing into the sky and firefighters and news crews were at the scene showing the devastation and the battle to get the fire under control. Nearby homes were being watered down to avoid the fire from spreading.

Fortunately the family was alerted by The Grinch and they fled to a safe location. Elvis had put some thought into this fire based on the reach it has. It was clearly arson. No explosions were heard meaning for someone to cause this much devastation in such a short time took planning.

The cameras scanned the crowd and Annie and I both saw Elvis with his arms folded watching what he did. He had no idea anyone was on to him. The police were getting close to finding the serial killer. Elvis was one of the police original person's of interest. They'll soon have him.

Elvis did one thing we hadn't expected. He left a letter at his apartment admitting to killing the two wives and the husband. He also exposed the CEO and his affair with his wife. This helped his wife with her lawsuit in the works the company didn't know about yet. It forced the CEO to step down immediately when the news came out, they had to protect the company from bad publicity, however, it was already too late.

All this was uncovered and Elvis, who killed three people, would never know about the CEO stepping down and his wife's winning lawsuit in the millions because his life ended that night.

Fortunately for us, we collected our payment before the police found the letter and confirmed he was the serial killer. The $1.5 million payment to us could not be explained from the debits in their accounting. They really couldn't say anything or they would have been sent to prison for life. Hiring anyone to kill someone is a felony in every law book. They would live with the civil suit loss as their only penalty.

Chapter 38

I talked it over with Annie and she agreed to accompany me to Texas. I promised I would make it a fun couple of days and we could wrap things up with the house. She could bring Bridgette and/or Holly along. Maybe do their favorite thing called Shopping. I also contacted the Gertz's asking if I could visit them when I'm in town. They were happy to hear from me and said of course.

I called the realtor and told him I'd be in town tomorrow and if we could meet around noon it would be perfect. He agreed to the time and called it a plan. I contacted the airport and made plans to have the jet ready by 8 a.m. the next morning. They have a service that provides a pilot and a staff if needed. Candy had been my pilot for recent trips. I really liked her service.

Morning came and all the girls met me at the airport before 8 a.m. I told them go easy on the luggage they bring since I knew they would be shopping. We were in the air on time and once again, Candy was our pilot and the co-pilot was Buzz again. I learned he got his name in the air force for his propensity to fly between tall buildings and buzzing the people on the ground much to the dismay of the military brass.

Annie walked over to me and planted a big old kiss on my lips. I could never get enough of that. It was early but that didn't stop the Bridgette and Molly from an alcohol fortified breakfast. Soon after, Annie and I joined in for some liquid refreshment. The ladies were having some girly conversation while I looked at paperwork the realtor faxed me about the possibility of renting the house.

We touched down smoothly and this time I had a limo pick us up and take us to the house. Bridgette and Molly had never seen so much grass, white fencing and horse farms before. It really felt like the sticks. We passed through town, their so called city and eventually reached our destination. After we settled in and unpacked, I sent the three ladies back to Houston for some shopping.

I had the real estate agent come pick me up and take me to the office and get my copies. We discussed our options in case things changed and I didn't move there. I did buy it at a discount because of the speed of settlement, a cash purchase and the fact that they had the property for sale more than 8 months. It really wasn't completely about the money. The house can just be an investment.

We talked options. If I were to resale the property, I could finance it myself (best option) or at a discount I could accept with terms to move it quickly. I could rent it and his real estate company could manage the property leaving it hands free for me. I would pay for any repairs and pay the managing fee, a percentage of the rent. I did have another alternative in mind that I was checking into later.

He brought me back to the house, we shook hands and he returned to his office or another property. While the ladies were still shopping, I moved to the next item on the agenda. I knocked on the door of the Gertz's. With a smile on her face, Marie welcomed me in. Frank came over to shake my hand.

We knocked out the chit chat and I asked them how their daughters were doing. "Pretty good I think. I know Becky is struggling a little and Ann Marie was happy where she was." I explained, "There is a possibility I might not be able to move in the house anytime soon and that I'm considering renting it or offering a rent to own opportunity for the right family. The terms would be favorable to avoid adding any stress of a high payment." It could be an investment property.

Frank jumped in, "Becky had been hinting about moving back," he added. I'm not sure when or how serious she is at this time." Marie commented, "It sure would be nice to have her near." "I wanted to ask you first because you two have been here since the beginning and I think it would be nice if had a good neighbor move here."

"'I'll tell you what, I'm not making any decisions until I hear from you. If Becky doesn't want to move here maybe someone from church or another neighbor might know of someone." "Again, no rush, I will be here for two days and I'll give you my number if you have any questions."

"That really sounds nice Tom (My cover name in Texas). Thank you," Marie said. Giving her a hug and Frank a handshake, I walked back to the house. There is still no sign of Annie and company. I gave her a call to see what they were up to and reminded her that her cover name here is Samantha. That could be tricky around Bridgette and Molly. I didn't think that one through when Annie invited them at my urging.

Annie answered, "Hey honey, what's up?" "Nothing much, before I forget, remember you cover name in this neighborhood is Samantha and I'm finished with business, any idea when you're coming home?" "We'll probably be done in about 2 hours and then head back." "Ok, I have dinner plans scheduled for later." "Sounds good honey, see you soon."

I took a shower and relaxed until I heard the Limo arrive. Once again they had about a dozen bags. When they came inside, I said, "OK ladies, I expect a fashion show tonight!" They laughed and Molly said, "Can you handle it Mr. Bill?"

I said, "No problem." Bridgette looked at me put her finger in her mouth and seductively pulled it out slowly across her lips. That sure had my imagination going. These girls are so unpredictable.

Everyone had their best outfits on. I had the Limo prepared for a ride to Morton's the Steakhouse in town for dinner. Donny, the Limo driver came into the house and took the 5 bottles of champagne and ice into the limo for our ride to and from. After final inspections in the mirrors, everyone was ready and we jumped into the Limo.

I know the Limo was a bit much watching all the onlookers checking to see what was going on. After all, as far as I knew, it was a small neighborhood and probably has never seen a Limo except once or twice for very special occasion. What I do believe is it further added to our cover.

We popped three bottles of champagne and made many stupid toasts with sarcasm toward each other. Toasts like;"To the best 3 dick magnets I know." "To the Limo driver who thinks on time is having a period." "To teasing Bill tonight when we get home"

"To Santa who said to his wife, Yes I went to my old girlfriend's house, it's my job you idiot." "To getting no snow at Christmas on the beach." "To giving up on figuring out what a woman wants,"

This is the short list. After all, at least we had excuses to celebrate. We had a buzz when we were being seated for dinner. We ordered our drinks and looked over the menu. I was all about the filet mignon with mushrooms. Annie had shrimp and scallops, Holly the same. Bridgette had the lobster and shrimp. I ordered an extra steak and some pork chops for takeout.

"Ladies enjoy your dinner. Tomorrow we go clubbing before we leave town." "Thank you," Molly and Bridgette said simultaneously.

I sometime think they have twin brains. It's uncanny how often they talk in stereo.

After dinner, we sat around for a while discussing stories from their experiences in the club. I use the term fall in lust about the guys in my Limo every night. They get such a kick out that line.

They talked about how the ladies reel them in and depending on whether they are cute or not, they sometimes feel sorry for them, determining how much money they will let them spend. All the dancers have their own ways of handling their business. Some just hang out to lure the big catch (The man with big money).

Some rub their boobs into their faces and read the reaction to get a lap dance or more importantly a private dance. I could tell you a lot more about their powers, maybe some other time. Remember it's strictly business, nothing personal.

I make the joke all the time, we live in the Bible belt and can't get a casino to help solve the financial woes from seasonal ups and downs and yet there about 140 strip clubs in North and South Carolina combined.

That's enough conversation analysis. Donny was waiting out front to bring us back. We popped the last two bottles and finished them by the time we got home. I tipped Donny and let him go back to his office. We had a fashion show about to make my day.

The girls were all giddy getting ready. Bridgette was first to come out of the bedroom. She had on a Victoria Secrets silk teddy in black with white trim in the shape of a heart. The rib area had puffed material adding depth to the outfit. She wore some new stiletto healed black leather boots. She moved over to me and teased me with a 10 second lap dance.

Next Molly came out in a pair of bright pink short shots, naked up top and a pair of white stiletto boots and a pink cowgirl hat. I could see her in this at the club getting a rise out of all the guys. She too came to me and teased me with a 10 second lap dance with the extra tease of boobs in my face.

Finally, out came Annie. She was wearing very a sexy lacey brazier and panties. She had on a black leather pair of boots with a silver decoration around the top of the leather. I did get a 30 second lap dance from Annie while Molly and Bridgette kept making obscene gestures in fun.

The fashion show was a blast. They really know how to put on a show every time. Annie and I took our fashion show private and Bridgette and Molly took theirs to the other bedroom. It was a very good night.

Chapter 39

That phone call last night, was from The Grinch. He had another job for us to handle. I had to be careful to keep the files away from Molly and Bridgette from viewing any of our assassin work. I had Donny pick up the girls and take them to town from some lunch while I took care of some family business from New York. Wink, wink. I told them I would be done by the time they got back and we could make plans to hit some night clubs later.

Donny picked them up and I had peace and quiet. I downloaded the dossier and went to work. The client was a scorned wife, Monica Star, who found out both her family money she brought to the marriage was squandered by her lousy husband Jacob Star.

He had a bad gambling problem and on several occasion had participated in affairs that turned out were caught on video and photos from the private detective she hired. It hurt to learn of the lies, indiscretions and lack of respect to her. Now there are blackmail threats to top it off, extorting money from him.

Jacob was the quintessential con man. He had been living off the weaknesses of women his whole life. The Stars were married for 25 years having celebrated their anniversary in a big public celebration party a few months ago. To their friends and the outside world, it appeared a great marriage. As it happens so often, the marriage was a front covering up the many problems the marriage had.

She knew for years about the other women. What she didn't know was how he used false accounting records to hide his mishandling of the couples and company's funds. If she didn't stop this soon, she would lose everything she inherited, nearly 10 billion from her dad when he passed many years ago.

Her husband ran the business and treated it like it was his personal ATM. A yacht, private plane and private condos in various cities around the world were some of the possessions he accumulated.

Their main residence was in Greenwich Village. They had several other vacation homes in Hawaii, Florida, San Francisco and Chicago she knew about. She was so spoiled most of her life, she never worried about money. However, taking notice of her husband's liberties lately, she was out for revenge.

Long talks with her lawyer and accountant made the danger of losses real. It was all because her husband who did as he pleased causing her to hire a private detective and see the full extent of the situation. Her blood pressure boiled having all the evidence in front of her.

The options weren't promising. Divorce, have him removed from the company, maybe freeze the funds were among the discussions. The private detective had some connections that made people disappear. That caught her attention. She was very interested and yet concerned it might be a setup.

The private detective became a good friend, a very private friend she could trust since her dad died. She told him about everything including her options and eliminating her husband. She truly knew she could trust this man. He convinced her to let him handle it and that they never had this conversation. That's when The Grinch was contacted and arrangements made.

We knew Jacob had an eye for the ladies. He liked rich women who kept quiet. He sometimes used a service called the GFE Request Agency. Getting close to him made sense using this agency. If a problem occurred with any of the experiences, both the John and the service denied everything as confidential and left no paperwork trail.

Mostly cash transactions and no receipts was the mode of operation. If you wanted to use credit cards, you could if it was a prepaid card. Once you were in, you get a pass code to use going forward. If you called and wanted to stay anonymous, you used a burner phone.

Only finger prints, video, pictures and DNA on clothing could get someone eventually caught. The business did not offer sex. It was a legitimate business but flourished because of the privacy it kept.

In the dossier, the information showed Jacob had a scheduled date in two days at 7 p.m. with Mitzy. The plan was to switch Annie with Mitzy by being there early and getting him to think Annie was Mitzy and then I needed to get close enough to him to inject the EOL.

I was a little worried because Annie might have to play out the GFE to make it all seem natural. I in turn would have to have a GFE with Mitzy for the same reason. I'll discuss it with Annie later.

Chapter 40

The girls came back from lunch and were in great spirits. They kept talking about last night's playful times. We all had a blast, was the overwhelming consensus. "There is plenty of time before we go out to the clubs in town. We leave at 8 giving ya'll plenty of time to get dolled up," I told them.

Annie turned on the stereo and found a local station that played their favorite pop mix of songs. Bridgette and Molly started dancing to the music and Annie grabbed the vibrator pretending it was a microphone and lip-synced the words. When the first song was over, I brought out a tray of cocktails and they each grabbed one. Another party night has just begun.

Each of them took turns getting a shower and the music played on with a few commercials here and there. They shared the makeup and outfits and never stopped talking about I don't know what and I didn't really want to know. I showered and got dressed in my room before stepping out into an empty living room.

They were still getting ready. It took me about 15 minutes. They've been at it for an hour and half. No comment! Molly came out in her very pink short shorts and a pink flowing blouse with her pink cowgirl boots. Her red hair and cowgirl hat was a dick stopper. There is no way in the world you can't look and not stop in your tracks to stare at this beauty.

Bridgette had a black hip hugging leather dress on with her black stiletto boots. There was a little silver shimmer in the dress as she moved in any direction. With her long black hair, she looked like she was from Texas.

When Annie came out, I was in lust all over again. She had on a Christmas red short skirt and a bright white boob hugging low cut top with long sleeves. She also wore her stiletto heeled boots. I wanted to keep her home and attack her all over again....But I promised a night out.

Donny was waiting outside. I grabbed a bottle of Grey Goose and Petron for the ride out to the clubs and some orange juice, coke and ginger ale as a mixer. Inside the Limo, we cranked up the music, had the oscillating neon lights in motion, and grabbed a glass and the ice. Donny got then started with quick Petron shots before adding a mixer.

We had VIP seating at the top night club in Houston, Texas Badass, formerly the legendary Club 69. Top DJ's around the world showcase their remixes here and their DJ prowess. Big name music stars and many legends of past years still play and visit here.

Arriving at the front doors in a Limo brought all the eyes in the long line out front, looking in our direction. The venue from the outside was very impressive. All we cared was about the experience.

Everyone wanted to know who was in the Limo since many stars come to Texas Badass. The three ladies led the way and cameras were flashing like paparazzi after a major scoop.

We walked to the front of the line four across and arm in arm. There was no red carpet but I would imagine it would feel something like this. After all, I was just a Limo driver and the ladies were three strippers, excuse me, exotic dancers form Myrtle Beach.

We cleared the bouncers and were greeted by a pretty young lady who took us to our section in the loft. Our VIP section holds ten people. I'm sure we'll make some friends real soon. The crowd continued to pile in and it was almost time for the live show. There was music playing to fill the spacious room.

The Grey Goose and Petron started the girls buzz in the Limo and now it was time to raise it a notch. I had champagne at our table and the waiter took individual drink orders. He was dedicated to serving us I promised him he would be well taken care of and gave him 3 C notes as a tip to get his attention. It worked well and we never waited for a drink all night.

The DJ was given an award winning introduction and played for an hour nonstop. Hi energy cuts just the way I like it. He blended one hit after another and was on fire. The crowd was dancing like they were on speed or some other drug; some probably were, with the light show filling the venue adding to the electric atmosphere.

We had several VIP guests from nearby come visit us and dance with the girls. I had the three most gorgeous women in the club and they were the center of attention. Molly and Bridgette had some hot dance moves and riled up several dudes.

Bridgette and Molly started kissing each other making even a larger impression. Several of the guys were lucky enough to find their body's pressed against the ladies while dancing. Some even enjoyed kisses and then they were sent away.

The girls knew the power they have and loved to tease guys. This was the perfect forum for that. Annie was not into all the drama tonight. She sat on my lap with her arm around my neck and planted the occasional kiss. It was perfect. She was perfect. I know she deals enough with lusty hungry guys at the club back home. She wanted the BFE tonight and I could do that.

When the DJ stopped, another introduction came out and a pretty singer came on stage. She started singing her song and the DJ added the mix and those on the dance floor started jumping up and down like lunatics. I was that person once upon a time. I recognized the song from the radio but it was so loud, I didn't hear who Annie said it was.

Hours later, I was pretty drunk and the girls had a great night. We agreed it was time to go. I settled my tab and as promised, took care of the waiter. He cleared the way so we could weave through the crowd. Donny got my message and was waiting for us. I had originally planned to go club hopping but tonight we went home.

Chapter 41

I got up earlier than the girls. Lifting Annie's leg off mine, I put on some clothes and took a walk to see if Marie and Frank were available. It was only 10:30 which is early for me but I was sure they were up. I knocked on the door twice before Frank opened and invited me in. I explained I was leaving today and I was wondering about their daughter's plans.

They smiled and Marie told me about Becky. She wanted to move back if the house was still available. I told her I thought it was great and it's hers if she wants it. I would have the real estate agent get the paperwork to her and he would be managing my property. She could make the check out to his company. As a bonus, the first month was free and she only needed one month's rent deposit.

"I have to get back to Samantha and catch our plane. The house is furnished. If she wants to replace anything inside, she needs to have it put in storage and to coordinate that with my agent," I told her. I might have assassinated her son, but I really like the family and they had no idea of her son's past. I want to spread some good karma to them. They didn't need to know.

Donny was ready for our final Limo trip to the airport. There were no traffic issues to deal with and our jet was ready. Candy and the staff were there to greet us. The flight was smooth and soon we were arriving in Myrtle Beach. We did a lot in 48 hours and had some good times. I told Annie about the new job and to meet me at my house later to discuss the information and plan.

I had the dossier spread out over my kitchen table to see if I missed anything. Annie was on the way. I had to get focused because tomorrow we would be in Greenwich. I had convinced myself the GFE (Girlfriend Experience) switch was the safest and quickest way to get this done.

Annie came in and she looked over everything I had laid out. She saw my notes about the switch. She did think of meeting them in a restaurant they were going to eat at. That could be plan B if we miss our opportunity on the initial meet and greet. Annie would wear a revealing outfit to capture his attention in either location.

We made plans to land in Westchester County Airport. A rental car had been reserved nearby at the airport. The meeting place was the lobby in the Delamar Greenwich Harbor Hotel lobby. From there, he would take Mitzy to dinner. My hope is he will be early and I have time to meet him. Mitzy had black hair and Annie was wearing a black wig to match her appearance.

The rest of the description was HOT and Annie had that covered. We actually arrived at the hotel about 6:45. We were very early and that was a good thing. More time to determine the best views of each of their arrivals. The terrace seemed to be the best place to meet. The terrace offered a view of the harbor giving us a place to start with drinks and make plans for dinner.

The moment was drawing near. Annie stood on the opposite side of the room to be the wandering eye distraction and thinking he might believe Annie was Mitzy. From the dossier, the photo of the very handsome man looked exactly like the man who walked up to the bar. No signs of Mitzy yet.

I started moving in his direction and caught his attention by staring at Annie as if she was some eye candy I couldn't avoid looking at. Now he noticed her too. I waived to her to come get a drink. Jacob was only 10 feet away. I walked to where the bartender was getting a drink for Jacob.

I leaned forward appearing to be asking the bartender, but wanting Jacobs' attention and asked loudly, "Any good suggestions for fine dining nearby?" The bartender said, "We have some very good food here." I looked at Jacob, "I want to treat my date to a fantastic dinner, any recommendations?" Jacobs said, "Sure, The Rebecca and the Thomas Henkelmann are two of my favorites."

"Thanks, "I said reaching out to shake his hand and Annie walked up to us. He did the proper thing and shook my hand and I gave my usual firm handshake. "Hey honey, this nice gentleman gave me a couple of restaurants to have a nice dinner at." "Great, thank you sir," she said. Jacob smiled and we smiled in return.

Walking out of the bar area, Mitzy was crossing our path looking around for her boyfriend for the night. I thought, how bold was this husband to do all this in the city he lived in. Their marriage must have been over for some time or he is a real asshole. Enjoy it buddy. This is your last date.

Fortunately the EOL was in his blood stream and his 24 hour timer was counting down. I took the bartenders advice and ordered some food on the patio overlooking the harbor. A steak for me and salmon for her were simple orders. "Great choices," the waiter said. We wanted to get back to our plane after dinner and get back to Myrtle.

We were so glad to be home. A quick dip in the pool and hot tub and the latest flick on TV with Annie next to me was the perfect calm after the storm. We have been on a hectic schedule recently. It's been fun, crazy and stressful with the jobs we completed.

Chapter 42

My Limo client tonight was a Russian dude who loved his big game poker games. My job was to pick up 8 players including him. They lived in Murrells Inlet, Surfside Beach, three in Myrtle, Market Commons, Carolina Forest and Little River. It took nearly two hours to gather them all up.

Once all were accounted for, they directed me to the host house. A houseful of beautiful young ladies were there attending to their food and drink needs as if they were waitresses. On the trip to the house, I heard conversations of heavy gambling on sports from the previous weekend and upcoming games.

I think in $5 to $20 bets unless I'm on a job. They ranged from hundreds to tens of thousands gambled. I don't ask but I was curious to know who gambles this much. How could that many people gamble with reckless abandon? With my assassin earnings I could afford it now but I would hate to lose. When I'm spending my money, it's to have a good time and buy things of value like the plane, a house, help charities, etc.

My job was to wait outside and take the losers home. They started coming out about an hour later. I learned it was a $100.000 buy in. That would mean the winner would walk away with $800,000. It was the winner's duty to pay for the Limo at the end of the night.

Three of the girl's waitressing had boyfriends in the game. All the girls had a foreign accent. Not uncommon in Myrtle Beach anymore. Every year, foreign college students come to Myrtle and work in businesses throughout the Grand Strand. Most stay for 2 to 3 months. Some decide to live here permanently.

I could tell how pissed off the first loser was. The Limo was stocked with their coolers. He reached into a cooler for a beer and said something I didn't understand. He was the first and he won't be the last. He thanked me for the ride home and in his condo he went.

By the time I made it back to the house, three more had lost it all. This time I understood their murmurs coming from the back because only two spoke English. They all grabbed beers and asked for a stop to get cigarettes.

They smoked one at the convenience store because we don't allow smoking in the Limo. One guy complained he wanted to smoke and they allow it in Vegas. I told him he needs to go to Vegas or buy the friggin' Limo jokingly and they all laughed.

The final four lasted much longer unless they stayed around to watch the game unfold. I started picking them up at 7 and it was now midnight. They were paying me $150 an hour plus a 20% gratuity so I just waited.

Finally at 2 they emerged from the house. The game was over and a trip to a private club I'd never knew existed was the next stop. I don't think it was a legal club because there was no reference to the address on the internet. They stayed there for an hour and came out with 4 ladies.

"Driver, please drive around for an hour and then return here," said one of the older dudes. They brought a couple of vodka bottles and some red bulls. They put up the divider and the music playing club music came from one of their phones plugged into the auxiliary jack.

An hour passed and as instructed, returned to the club. The four ladies came out and 6 more came in. "Same thing, one hour again, thanks," the older dude said again. It would have been cool to have a camera in the back for curiosity sake but I was better off not knowing.

Again, an hour passed and as instructed, I returned to the club. This time the six ladies came out and I was instructed to take everyone to his house in Surfside. Finally I thought to myself, I'm almost done. The chatter in the back was too low for me to hear much.

We reached his house and everyone stepped out grabbing the coolers and other liquor remaining. The older man paid the Limo balance and a healthy tip. He was the big winner. I got the impression it wasn't his first big win. The back of the Limo was trashed. At least they paid me well to get it cleaned. I'll just pay a detailer tomorrow and go home for now.

Chapter 43

A big scandal hit the news regarding the Star's and their company. Jacob, the husband, was found dead in a call girl's condo belonging to Isabelle Capone in New York on last night due to a heart attack. That was the main thing I needed to hear. The headline story goes something like this.

Jacob loved more than the girlfriend experience. He paid for high priced hookers and when the police checked his pockets, they found his little black book that showed a schedule of meetings, how much he paid with names and numbers. The unidentified service was under investigation and arrests were being made by the dozens including Madam Chelsea, the owner.

Found in the hookers condo was a hidden video camera and a stash of SD cards with numerous videos of other prominent Johns who were being blackmailed. This was a future movie about to happen. Further evidence showed Jacob was a regular visitor of Isabelle's. Evidence also showed Jacob would conduct business offering happy endings to some of his clients.

Monica Star who paid for the hit was a piece of work in her own right. The news story revealed the phone calls to the detective and notes with photos of her husband's infidelity. She also wrote down her plans to have him killed in a notebook in her safe. Why leave such damning evidence. She's truly not the brightest bitch in town.

In her ledger found by the police, it has her saying she encouraged Jacob to have an affair years ago in attempt to orchestrate a divorce. Jacob took it to heart and never stopped. He embezzled millions form the company and had over 20 condos he used for affairs and put his favorite ladies in. Isabelle was one of those that were off the books. When she called 911, she had no idea the firestorm that would result.

Getting back to Monica, the police pursued the connection of the private detective and the plans to have her husband killed. All the police said was they are persons of interest and the investigation is ongoing. Same goes for Isabelle's blackmailing scheme and the fools on the videos.

Fortunately for us, our payment was received up front and we avoided all the drama. As the jobs pile up, I get concerned that the wrong information could get in the wrong hands leading back to me. Fortunately, The Grinch has been steps ahead of any problems and off the radar to any connections. The use of EOL to appear as a natural heart attack has been a smart choice.

Our funds have already been added to our secret bank account. I have added several new accounts to spread make transfers to after each payment received. Annie and I have a nice nest egg growing for when we retire.

Chapter 44

Annie's birthday was coming up soon. I wanted to make this her best ever. Turning 28 only comes once. Ha-ha, I know each birthday only comes once. I sure didn't want to focus on the number but rather the celebration of my special lady, best friend and partner.

Tonight's crew was already in party mode. A beach front resort had weekly pool parties with cheap drinks, a DJ, plenty of jocks and bikini babes getting sunburned and drunk. Starting to drink at home from noon until now, 3 in the afternoon, battling gravity was a challenge. There were a dozen guys and gals in total and in their beach attire.

Two young ladies fell face first getting into the Limo. Everyone had a good laugh. This group was some of my regular college partiers. They hooked up a phone to the auxiliary cord and instantly became the DJ and this DJ had a quick trigger finger. He kept changing songs before it was half over and the others started booing him for his constant changing of the tunes.

He got the hint and we continued on to the resort. Several of their friends came up to the Limo to meet them at the front. Their level of intoxication and the heat made for some concern and I reminded them to keep hydrated with water. It probably fell on deaf ears. They planned on leaving at 6.

I went around the corner to grab some food to go and kill some time. I had to park off to the side because parking was limited and the Hummer Limo was way too large to get near the entrance. The steak and cheese with loads of cheese, onions, mushrooms, green peppers and tomato sub really hit the spot.   Adding a little Heinz catsup was the right touch for a great sub.

It was a messy sub so after I finished, I stepped into the resort to wash up.   At the sink next to me, one of the crew had hurled somewhere and was cleaning himself up.   He didn't even notice me and I let him be.   I wandered out to the pool slightly overdressed to check out the gang and the atmosphere.   Most of my group was in a battle playing basketball in the pool.

The ladies were busy showing off for the guys they met today.   It is amazing how skinny so many of them are.   At this point in their young lives, they are metabolism machines.   Eating like them today would immediately find a spot on my belly.   I try to work out regularly to keep the physique I have.   It's a lot of work I took for granted when I was younger like them.

They had a half hour to go.   A few ladies closer to my age were checking me out.   Just then, Jessica from the group said, "Come on Limo Bill, take off your clothes and jump in."   I might have been tempted if I had bathing suit on.   Boxers wouldn't cut it although I'm sure they didn't care.   "Thanks," I said.   "Maybe another time," I said with a laugh.

I didn't see it coming but the basketball came flying at my head and I ducked just in time only to lose my balance and fall against the young lady checking me out.   "Not bad, "she said.   "Not bad."   Slightly embarrassed, I winked at her and left the pool area.

Soon after the ball flying incident, they signaled to each other it was time to go.   The long afternoon of drinking and sun seemed to wear them out.   Within a mile of getting back, most of them had their eyes closed.

One prankster tied the strings of 2 bras together and dropped an ice cube on each of them startling them from napping and screaming pulling away from each other causing their boobs to be on display briefly, much to the approval of the others in the Limo.

The girls scrambled for their towels. Then they separated the bras and put them back on. It was a quick laugh that woke them all up. The music was turned back on; they started singing the words, jumping up and down in the seats. Girls were lap dancing the guys and some guy's lap danced the girls.

Back at their place, I helped them out of the Limo. Wet hugs from most of the girls left an imprint on my clothing. My relationship with my clients is more like friends since I see many of them quite often. If I wasn't an assassin, I could enjoy this more often. I get to see things I would never do and could never imagine possible.

Chapter 45

Tonight was movie night with Annie. There were a few choices for movies at the theater in Market Commons this week. We had dinner plans at 8 and a movie afterwards. For now, it was time to return the Limo and go home and get ready to pick up Annie.

I picked up Annie at her place. She was ready for some us time like I was. Our dinner reservation was at Big Daddy's Roadhouse Grill in south Myrtle. I had an urge for ribs tonight. The ribs there simply fell off the bone. The fresh bread and baked potato and salad were a little much. Annie had the salmon and I shared some ribs with her. She wanted Bleu Cheese dressing. I preferred Italian.

We had a conversation about the last couple of crazy weeks, about setting up the house for the Gertz's daughter Becky. Talked about our trip to Texas with Bridgette and Holly, and then having dinner in Greenwich. The fashion shows the girls put on and the wild night after. We are in a good place now in our relationship. Romance is part of our life. A little dysfunctional at times but we know how to have fun.

The manager came over to check on us and say hello. I bring him golfers during the season and he appreciates it. I've never had a bad experience at Big Daddy's. He brought us a sinful desert and finished our drinks before catching our movie.

We chose the Fast and the Furious part 6. It kind of describes our life the last two years. In particular, the last few months have been flying by for us. I've watched all the movies from this franchise dozens of times. We waited before getting popcorn after the large dinner. It's just not a movie without popcorn I thought. As fast we sat down, I went back for the popcorn.

The theater was packed and nowhere to hide. We took our seats in the back and started munching on popcorn. I looked around the theater and saw mostly guys by themselves. The few groups of girls came to see Paul Walker and there quite a few couples sprinkled among the seats.

These chairs are so comfortable. I put my arm around Annie and we watched the entire movie without getting frisky with one another. Tonight was to be calm and relaxing, a de-stressing night. The movie was great. The crowd kept mentioning different scenes while walking to the exits.

On the way to her place we stopped at Piggly Wiggly for some beer and snacks. We reached her place pretty quickly and I joined her inside. We grabbed a couple of beers and sat on her balcony feeling the slight breeze and watching the moonlight. "Now that moon would look awesome on the water right now," I said. She smiled as if to say yes.

She brought up her dad and mom. "Dad was getting worse. He didn't even recognize me on the phone earlier when I called them. Alzheimer's sucks! I hate mom has to do so much for him." "I understand. She really loves him and wouldn't have it any other way. Don't you agree?" "Ya, I know, I wish I could help in some way." "Do you have anything in mind?" I said.

With her eyes on mine, "I think it's time to get professional help in the house. I don't want him to be in a home right now and I surely don't want to see him back in the hospital." I looked at her, "If there is anything I can do, don't hesitate to ask. You know we have plenty of money in our accounts." "I thought that was not to be touched," she said.

"The money is to be used for anything important and your family is very important. I see it in your heart." I added, "Besides, I used some of it for business investments, like the jet, the purchase of the house and there will be way more money coming in than what we'll spend in our lifetime if all goes well." "Our accounts are part of the business; we can use it for whatever we need."

"Let me talk to mom and ask her what we can do." "Absolutely, anything they need, we will make it happen, "I said. I could see that was important to her. I wrapped my arms around her and gave her a big kiss. We watched some cable tv and I stayed with her for the night. We lay in each other's arms until we fell asleep. I was happy to just be with her.

Chapter 46

The sun was rising in the east as I looked off the balcony. Annie walked up behind me and wrapped her arms around my waist. I put my arms on hers and soaked in the moment. She felt so good up against me. I could still smell her perfume and I laid my head back a little. After the discussion about her dad last night, I saw hurt and love I never noticed in her before.

I get so wrapped up in our complex lives, I don' take time to really look at all those around me. Annie was my babe. I vowed from this minute forward to pay more attention to how she is feeling. Despite my job, I had plenty of compassion for the emotional pain of others.

She said, "I'm taking a shower, want to join me?" "No need to tell me twice, I'm right behind you sweetie?" I followed her into the bathroom and watched her drop her satin robe. She undressed and so did I. Our bodies filled the small condo sized shower.

I pulled her lips to mine and we shared a powerful passionate kiss. Annie was a great kisser. We continued smooching under the shower head with water pouring on the top of our heads. It was like a game we played to see how long we could keep kissing with the pelting water.

I finally moved away to grab a bar of soap and reaching my hand around to her front, I ran the soap in sensual motions across her boobs, arms, abs, in between her legs and bent down to finish with her thighs and calves. Spinning around allowed the shower to rinse off the soap. She backed into me and pressed her ass cheeks against me.

She felt so good I moaned a silent pleasure. She then took the soap and lathered me up with special attention to get me excited. I couldn't help hide my excitement and she raised one leg high against the wall opening herself up for me to penetrate to please. We used her flexibility to have sex in the shower.

I reached down with some baby oil and massaged her hot spot until she let out a screech and moaned of pleasure. I never stopped massaging her entire body until she was ready to leave the shower. Talk about a wakeup call.

She had some errands to do giving me the hint to go home for now. I had a few things to do as well and I wanted to get to the gym today. After getting dressed, we kissed goodbye and took care of our agendas. I reminded her to call her mom and told her to stop over later so we could talk about it.

Annie came home after doing some shopping. I fired up the grill with some steak, chicken, corn on the cob and baked potatoes. Salad was made with all the fixings. Annie was on the phone with Bridgette talking shop. The club was expected to be busy tonight and all dancers were expected to work. Annie didn't have to be there until 8 or 9. I had a 10 o'clock pickup myself.

Chapter 47

Tonight was going to be interesting. I was referred by another Limo company who was overbooked. Business is business. We've referred back and forth a few times. When I made it to the Sheraton, I text them I was out front for the 10 o' clock reservation. There were three guys I shook hands with. Bob, Duane and Roger were their names.

Bob was dressed in slacks and a white shirt with no tie. He presented himself as a business man and you could just tell he was an executive of some type. Duane had on jeans and called himself Bob's executive assistant. I thought of him as the friend along for the ride and an excuse for Bob to be bad. Roger appeared to be a lower level manager of some type.

Myrtle Beach, like many cities that host conventions, gives the convention goers an opportunity to live a little and do things in another city they wouldn't do at home. It could be they are away from fellow employees, it could be gambling, it could be they are married or have a significant other left behind. It works the same for both men and women.

It's like an actor who likes to play the bad boy or bad girl that isn't there normal personality. Add alcohol and inhibitions are lowered, crazy and wild things can and do happen. This is one of those stories. Bob was married and the son of a wealthy business owner. He was following into his dad's footsteps and being groomed to take over the family business.

He loved the strip clubs and more the challenge to throw enough money to have his GFE with benefits. He was from the other side of the country so getting caught was unlikely, getting in trouble was very likely. There was no other choice but to go to a strip club. He'd heard others on the golf course mentioned The GFE Gentlemen's Club.

We were greeted by the valet and a few handshakes later they were inside. I parked the Limo around the corner and went inside to make sure he was happy there. I saw the wad of hundreds and estimated it at 5 to 6 thousand dollars. The three men had several ladies vying for their attention. One dancer was a certified porn star with over 100 videos to her credits.

He was tipping $20's when most guys tipped $1's and $5's. The word among the girls spread and now he had ten lovely ladies around his table and each guy had lady on each lap. He bought a bottle of bourbon for his table and a rack of jello shooters. He came to play and play hard tonight.

I left them there although my curiosity had me imagining what would happen in the private room. By 11:30, they were ready to leave. Bob found his new girlfriend for the night. Roger asked to be taken back to the hotel. It wasn't his scene. He was married and was feeling guilty after he pocket dialed his wife with all the loud music and ladies sweet voices in the background.

Duane's job was to help Bob be naughty and keep him out of trouble. On top of that, he wanted to go to a gay bar. He was more into the gay scene and hoped to have his night fulfilled. Bob and his shiny little playmate went to Broadway at the Beach. When I dropped Bob and his date off, Duane became three's company and stayed behind.

I took him to the gay bar, the Rainbow House and planned for a 1 a.m. pickup. I waited for a call from either of them and nothing. Finally I went to the Rainbow House and waited until 1 in the morning.

While I was waiting, I heard a window being broken and in my side mirror I watched someone break into a car and steal an iphone and laptop. He was quick. I called the police giving them the license number. The rest was up to them.

Duane never came out so I went inside looking for him. He was in an embrace with some dude. I had seven offers for a drink. I didn't get it right away. Then it hit me. I guess I should feel flattered. Duane yelled, "Be right out buddy!" It took about 15 minutes and then he came running out. Bob had called and wanted to be picked up now.

I was still wondering how he was able to get a dancer out of the club. It's against all rules for the girls. I thought maybe Bob bought her work time but even that never happens. Lots of people come with lots of money and I've never personally seen it happen before. I've known girls to give their numbers to a select few and meet after hours or the next day for lunch. Wink, wink.

We rushed to Broadway and pulled up in front the Hard Rock Café. Duane noticed Bob and waved him to us. The girl was still all over him. Duane sat up front with me and Bob and his date got in the back. After closing the door, we pulled off and he wanted to go back to the Sheraton.

My curiosity still bothering me, I asked Duane about Bob and how he got the girl. It turns out the girl was a friend of a dancer and the two hit it off. Now that made sense. Still, it seemed very easy. Reaching the hotel, everyone exited and Bob paid me the balance of the deposit and tipped me decent. He handed me his business card and thanked me. We shook and they left.

When I got home, I reached in my pocket finding the business card. Why not I thought, I checked his company on the internet. His dad had built a huge commercial real estate holding empire. Bob was the son and listed as executive vice president. He was to take over the business in a few years. The net assets for the company were 53 billion dollars.

That's Billion with a B. What do you do with that much money? Not that I would mind having it but that's a lot of dough. I'm not worried. I'm building my little fortune one job at a time. I look forward to the day I can retire and find ways to spend it while I'm still relatively young and with my Annie.

Chapter 48

While I was day dreaming about our future, The Grinch notified me and I was to learn of someone who wasn't going to have one.   A dossier was on the way for my next job. I was on my way home and now I had to start making plans after learning who my next target was. Annie was still at work so I sent her a text asking to come over for lunch.

According to the dossier, a George Masterson was my target. Masterson ran a child abduction scam.   He's been operating in Canada for several months now and has orchestrated the abduction of three young boys under the age of 2. All three abductions happened in public areas. A mall, a park and at the Canadian side of Niagara Falls.

The authorities have followed leads but nothing has even come close to finding the children. They don't really have a suspect yet. Lots of speculation and a long tip line but nothing solid. The father of little Joey was the only parent contacted. He was very rich and a ransom demand was made.

He cooperated with the FBI but immediately hired his own group of specialized detectives to do what they do.   All the research and questioning by the detectives led them to the state of Michigan. Looking specifically for child abduction for sale, they found dozens of leads. Money was not an obstacle for the father of the child. One person of interest is Masterson. He's been questioned in the past.

What they learned through the army of private detectives is the ransom contact was perpetrated from an office building in Flint

Michigan where Masterson worked as a legitimate business person. That is where Masterson works. David Hicks, the farther of Joey, remembered his voice on the ransom demand when one of his detectives recorded him with surveillance equipment.

Next step is to follow his every move and tap his phone including his cell phone. A couple of days later, he made the mistake of being heard discussing he had 5 little kids ready for sale. Bingo. Now they had something to work with. David Hicks contacted the FBI and informed them what they had heard and who should be the main focus.

A complete task squad was on top of it now. Back in Canada, police were following up on leads from the other end of the phone call. The goal now was to get him to lead the FBI to the children. A second ransom call came to Mr. Hicks. The demand was for $2 million. He would call back with a location. David hoped his son was still alive.

Masterson made his next call instructing Jacobs to put the money in a black duffle bag and have it dropped on the roof top of the 3000 Town Center in Detroit. He warned if he saw any police, he would have his son killed and a bomb in a different building would go off killing many people. David pleaded to talk with Joey and all he said was trust him, telling him he has 12 hours to comply and he'll call again.

David had to get to Detroit with the money and see this threat through. He made it within an hour of the deadline. The FBI had the building covered. The call came and said, "I see you on the roof, now leave the bag there by the side where the other black bag is. Switch bags and take the bag down and go three buildings south and go to the top of that building.

The FBI saw Hicks going to the other building. The units shifted to the building Hicks went into. When he reached the top, he found his little boy was tied to a pole on top. A helicopter flew over the first building with the money and Masterson, who collected his money grabbing the hanging ladder and he disappeared in minutes. The FBI didn't react in time to catch him.

Fortunately, the private detectives had anticipated the helicopter and had video feed on the roof. They taped Masterson and the helicopter with all of its identification numbers. With a tracker on the money both by the FBI and the detectives, Masterson had a small window to get away. Choppers were in the air tracking the money and zeroed in on his whereabouts.

With a massive search on the ground and in the air, Masterson and the money was captured. He was interrogated for hours about the other missing children. He kept asking for a deal if told them where to find them. Running out of time, they agreed to a plea bargain if they rescued the children alive.

He gave them the location and they found 6 children under the age of 3 being held hostage by two men left as scapegoats. Masterson wanted his payday and planned to disappear with his new riches. He got greedy and it got him caught. After the children were found, the FBI believed there were some already sold and offered a larger plea bargain for additional children.

When it was all said and done. 17 children were located and returned to their thrilled families. It was a happy ending from a dark possibility. Masterson would be in a light security prison per the plea bargain for the deals he did. There was no possibility for parole. The only thought Hicks had was the possibility of a breakout and he wanted to Masterson to pay for his sins.

That's where I come in. Masterson was to die. David Hicks, our client, wanted this to happen soon. With Masterson in prison, there was no way I could get close enough to him and not be a person of interest after his death. I work too hard to stay off the radar.

Annie was looking over the dossier again and the situation of Masterson in prison. She agreed with my analysis. Going to visit him in prison was way too much risk. I needed to touch base with The Grinch. He needed to be aware of my concerns and give him the only option I could come up with.

It was the first time I ever talked to The Grinch directly. He heard what I had to say as my only solution I could agree to and be a part of this. He said to give him time to contact his client and examine any alternatives.

The client agreed, as a matter of fact, he wanted it this way. He wanted to be the person to get justice and assure the world would never have to worry about Masterson again. He would be terminated. The plan I had was to send him an EOL drug and for him to administer the drug to Masterson.

This came with a detailed set of instructions on how administer one dose of EOL and make sure he doesn't accidentally inject himself. I'm uncomfortable letting this in anyone else's hands but this is a unique situation. I get to remain unidentified and stay incognito. That is imperative. No one will suspect the drug in a band aid form

Hicks received the EOL and the detailed instructions. He lined up a meeting at the prison and acted as though he forgave him. He came face to face with him and guards all around. He said, "Thank you for not harming my boy and helping all the other children get saved." He reached his hand out to give him a handshake. In his cuffs, he shook his hand and Hicks gave him the firm hand shake,

Hicks smirked and turned around and walked out. Masterson was trying to talk to him but Hicks just kept walking. He disposed of the

EOL strip as instructed and felt the weight and anger leave his body. In 24 hours, Masterson would be in hell where he belonged.

News of Masterson's death was a blurb on the nightly news. Dying with a heart attack was not as interesting as getting killed in a prison fight or attack. He won't be costing the taxpayers for the next 30 years if he lived that long. The incident brought the Hicks family closer than ever together. David Hicks never missed a ball game, science project or any event in his family's life.

Chapter 49

It was time for a poolside cookout. I invited many of the locals who hired me in the past and told Annie to invite anyone she wants. I asked her if she heard back from her mom yet and her answer was not yet. Of course the usual crowd of Allan and his friends, Bridgette, Molly and their friends. We also sent invitations to our friends who worked at restaurants, hotels, resorts and bars if they had the day off.

I had two trash cans of ice and beer. There was plenty of liquor for shots and mixed drinks. Fresh beach towels and tiki lights were part of the décor. Dozens of hot dogs, burgers, chicken strips, chips, pretzels and water to keep hydrated with all the alcohol were on the menu. I had the taxis on notice for later.

We did the prep work and soon we'll see who can make it. Many are working and plan to stop over if the party is still going. Food would be served from 8 o'clock on. Annie and I relaxed in the hot tub prior to everyone showing up.

The first knock on the door and it was Allan with his new girlfriend Jade and 4 of his good friends from work. They all worked the day shift and got out early. Minutes later Molly and Bridgette walked up to the front door. Two other cars pulled up and the party was officially on. Everyone got the memo of bathing suits.

In less than an hour we had nearly 30 people for the cookout and party. We all took turns keeping the grill full of good eats. Nearly everyone had a drink in their hands, conversations were taking place at the pool, the hot tub, on the deck, inside the house and some were walking on the beach with their toes in the water.

It was a crescent moon tonight glistening on the water and the stars filled the clear skies. The sight of the night sky was truly majestic. The cool breeze on a rather humid night was a welcomed relief. I could see Annie and Molly laughing about something someone said. She turned her head to me and smiled. I never get enough of her smile.

Everyone had their fill of food by now. It was time for our shot games. I had a Vegas styled wheel with 24 different slots, each with a drink command. It's a rather unique party game. Here is the colorful shot list:

- Absolute shot
- Purple Hooter shot
- Jagermeister shot
- Pornstar shot
- Choose one person to spin twice
- Choose who you want to drink a shot off your belly
- Choose whose belly you want to drink off of
- Choose whose bikini top you want to do a tube shot from
- Swallow 2 shots of your choice
- Sex on the Beach
- Alabama Slammer shot
- B-52 shot
- Screaming Orgasm shot
- Blow Job shot
- Buttery Nipple shot
- Lemon Drop shot
- Tequila shot
- Russian Quaalude shot
- Redhead Slut shot

-     Everyone gets a shot of your choice, you must take 2 shots
-     Petron shot
-     Liquid Cocaine shot
-     Pussy Potions shot
-     Leg Spreader shot

Pretty simple rules, every person in the crowd gets a number to take their turn. Everyone has an Absolute shot simultaneously to kick off the game. The game should end after 6 spins (optional). Once completed, everyone takes a simultaneous shot ending the shot game.

There was bartender ready to be the shot maker. I started it off and landed on the Buttery Nipple shot. The crowd chanted my name until I drank my shot. Cheers and chants from the crowd continued into round three. By now, people were getting silly and talking trash to one another. Besides the shots, everyone was still partaking of their drink of choice.

On Molly's fourth spin, she landed on choose a bikini top to drink a shooter from. She chose Bridgette as we anticipated and they had some fun with it as her top came off and Molly's lips were all over her sumptuous breasts. It was a sight to see and added another story to the crazy night.

This continued until round 6 finished, the final group of random shots laid out on the bar for those still playing the game was swallowed simultaneously ending the shot game per the rules. It was nearly midnight by now. Many had work the next day and began their farewells if they had a designated driver. I has several taxi's ready to get everyone home safe. About a dozen remained and proceeded to the deck.

I closed off deck with the partitions and kept our party private from wandering eyes. Someone screamed out, "Skinny dipping time!" Everyone was in good spirits so I turned the lights off and everyone in the hot tub stripped naked. The hot tub was designed for 10 people max, but somehow all 12 fit tonight. The neon lights glowed in the hot tub.

We were a close group obviously. Seeing all the naked bodies was actually hilarious. I'm sure at some point they all skinny dipped in the past but I doubt it was with any of this group except maybe Annie, Bridgette, Molly and I. We've had a few moments in the past when we were very drunk just like tonight.

There were 7 ladies and 5 guys. It was impossible to not be in contact with the person next to you with so many of us squeezed in the hot tub. I had Annie sitting on my lap which took every ounce of will power not to just do her. Everyone started getting out about 30 minutes later. They grabbed towels to dry off and found their bathing suits.

The bartender was staring at the beautiful ladies and their full nudity. Seeing them was a better tip than any cash I could offer. When I paid him at the end of the night, he offered to do our next cookout with a smile. I chuckled saying, "I don't blame you dude. I'll be in touch." He did a good job particularly with the shot game.

The night finally ended as everyone left except Molly and Bridgette who stayed the night since they were too drunk to drive and already had some clothes in the guest bedroom. This party will be talked about in many circles for some time, certainly until the next party when new stories will happen.

Chapter 50

I was scheduled for another wedding with a pickup about 4 p.m. in Cherry Grove which is just north of North Myrtle Beach. The pickup was at The Prince Resort located at 3500 North Ocean Boulevard. The nuptials were being performed near the Cherry Grove Pier. The reservation was to pick up the wedding party. The newlyweds, five groomsmen and five bridesmaids were to be my honored guests.

I made it there for the wedding ceremony at 3:30 and was taken back by the crowd. My version of a wedding is everyone getting dressed up and the bride and groom looking the best they will probably ever look in her wedding dress and he in a suit or tux. I know there are many ways weddings are based on their lifestyles.

There are beach weddings in bare feet or sandals. I've seen weddings from ski slopes to cliff diving, parachuting, on horseback, in race cars, zipline weddings, paint ball, parasailing and a host of other creative ways. This wedding, well, it is a Redneck Wedding. There is no other way to describe it.

The bride had her wedding dress over her jeans and bare feet. The groom wore a camouflage outfit with a white bow tie, his fishing hat with fishing hooks and a permit attached and also going barefoot. The groomsmen had on white wife beater t-shirts and the bridesmaids wore jeans and a tee shirt that said "Danger Redneck Girls Do It Right"

The crowd was just as dressy. They were wearing jean overalls, outfits that showcased a multitude of tattoos on both the men and women. Over a dozen had can's for chew and either beer or moonshine. And this was the group I'm putting in my Limo.

Spectators were like paparazzi having a field day. I could only imagine the captions for those photos. I could never dream of a wedding like this but to each his own. When the ceremony finally reached "I DO," the crowd raised their beers in the air and two shotguns blasted from an unknown location.

This was my first and probably only shotgun wedding in the true sense of the word. The wedding party made their way onto the pier and then to the Limo. Strings with cans attached and hung from the back of the Limo. The reception was in the backyard of a beach house in Sunset Beach, North Carolina. I was rented for 4 hours. It was time to have a redneck time.

The wedding couple had their very own tattoo masters at the reception. After the toasting was done and they finished eating at the gourmet barbeque and deep fried chickens, the bride and groom had tattoos inked on each other.

The brides said, "Married to Jeff My One and Only Man." It had a fancy design in red all around it. Jeff's tattoo said, "Married to Lisa My One and Only Gal." It also had the same design in red all around it. The hip hop music was being played by the DJ with country music in some stretches blasted over the speakers.

It was a simple wedding with about 50 or so in attendance. I still hear the shotguns blasting in my head. I thought I was on a reality show of some type. Maybe I was because it really happened and I'm sure someone had it on video. This is one of those wild stories people ask me to tell them.

Time was moving on and the contract was nearing an end. I needed to load up all those going back to the Prince Resort. On the way back, the newlyweds were all over each other. It just looked odd to see the jeans on under the wedding gown. I was praying no one's spit missed their cans and cups used to collect their chew.

They couple had their honeymoon right there at the Prince Resort. They told me they have no plans to leave the room for 3 days. I'm going to guess that in nine months, baby number two will bless their future. I heard them talk about wanting another baby in the back of the Limo.

The bride gave me a big hug thanking me for making their day special. The new husband also gave me a big hug. Their special day had nothing to do with me. I was just the ride. They did it their way, very unconventional, but it was the way they planned probably for quite some time. I was told they dated for 5 years with many break ups and always made it back to each other.

There were so many laws broken today but it all worked out, starting with the shotgun going off, beer on the beach and cans hanging from the back of the Limo just to name a few. We weren't in redneck country where this might be more acceptable. I wonder how the honeymoon is going with the new tattoos freshly inked. It has to be painful in certain positions.

Chapter 51

The Grinch sent me new files for my next job. The mark was Harry Fenner. Mr. Fenner is a former patron of the New York State Penitentiary. He was convicted of raping a woman then beating her into a coma. Mandy Lentz, the victim stayed in a coma for nearly 3 years. The husband was devastated and wanted this man to pay for what he did to his wife.

Andy Lentz visited his wife every day at the hospital encouraging her to never give up. After nearly three years, Mandy showed some responsive movements. The doctors were encouraged and the miracle Andy hoped for seemed possible. Holding her hand on the hospital bed with all the monitors attached and beeping sounds repeating in the room, he kept praying.

She had moved her hand earlier in the day. All that hope disappeared in an instant. His prayers were interrupted by alarms going off and a mad rush of doctors and nurses. They were rushing her into the operating room and the nurses had to constrain Andy from following them. Mandy was going into cardiac arrest. Andy broke into tears. He was mentally exhausted with her battle.

It was a sad day for the victim of Fenner years ago. It wasn't fair he lived and she died that day. Andy Lentz vowed revenge for his wife. He didn't know how but that man was going to pay. He went to work every day at Wall Street doing his best to earn enough money to get his revenge against that son of a bitch. Rage consumed him and he was driven.

As time passed, Andy started to move on and the rage dwindled but his commitment to avenge his wife's death did not. His expertise in the market created a nice little next egg. He had earned nearly $10 million and still wasn't a happy man. He really loved his wife.

Two years passed since Mandy passed away. The New York State Penitentiary was having overcrowding issues and inmates who were near the end of their terms along with low level inmates stood a chance of being released. It was all over the news and Andy had his lawyer check into Fenner's disposition.

Fenner's name was on the list to be released in about a month. The wheels in Andy's head were turning. This was his chance to get revenge. He did so well in his business; he needed to find a way his business wouldn't be jeopardized. He learned of our services years ago through his previous lawyer. At that time, he was such a mess and couldn't afford the $1 million minimum.

With his current assets he's accrued, that was no longer a hindrance. He contacted The Grinch and an agreement was made, the corresponding dossier was sent to me. Annie came over and saw the story behind the job and was quite passionate about this job. Rapist pissed her off.

A couple of friends she knew had been raped and Annie herself was molested by a creepy uncle who mysteriously was run over by a car while on vacation. It was a hit and run never solved. She called it karma and karma can be a bitch. She knew the woman who was driving the car and never turned her in. It was silent justice.

Our private detective had plenty of details in the dossier. Who his friends and acquaintances were his family, previous employers, drug dealers nearby and where he frequently hung out before his arrest. The original case files showed several B & E's, multiple fights, a misdemeanor arrest for drugs and a rape arrest and his rape case was acquitted by the courts.

Fenner had the kind of past that leads to a personality unlikely to change. If he raped once and based on his past, the odds are he'll do it again. It might not happen right away but if he gets down on his luck just might be inclined to think, "What the F*&*!" This is a troubled soul who could damage another innocent victim's life.

We have to go to Albany, New York to locate Fenner and find our best opportunity to meet him and inject him with EOL. Time to fire up the jet and see what Albany has to offer. The jet was prepared and Annie and I packed for 2 days. We landed at Albany International Airport, picked up a rental car and got right to work.

We located the house listed in the dossier. It sure looked like a pretty tough neighborhood. In the dossier, Fenner had been known to frequent the local strip clubs. There were several to choose from. Fortunately, the dossier narrowed the options down to two locations. It was five years ago when Fenner was a free man. We traced his old ways but a lot has changed.

What hasn't changed is the drug dealers listed still existed. Our private detective was also here to support us. I had a conversation with the detective and he said Fenner was working as a dish washer for a local restaurant. He learned it was cash under the table kind of job from an old family friend. We stayed near his house and the detective's job was to follow him from the job.

I received a call he was done work and at a convenience store by his house. He couldn't tell for sure but it looked like a transaction was going down on the side of the building. His guess was some drugs or a weapon. He didn't have a history of weapons leaving us to bet on drugs.   Fenner walked to his place and the detective staked his apartment out.

It was a house that had multiple apartments for rent inside. I was surprised a building like this wasn't condemned.   Small drug purchases like weed, coke, meth, crack, and oxycontin were favorites among individual users and abusers. This was the place to go for local drug addicts.

We went to our hotel for the night staying on alert from the detective. The hotel was only a few miles away. If there was any movement, we needed to know right away. We all focused on ending this as soon as possible.

Our big break finally came. He came outside and started walking toward the strip clubs. Annie and I rushed over immediately and actually passed him before the parking lot. I found a spot away from the outdoor camera's view. He had about 1000 feet to go. I rolled my window down and when he came near, I asked him, "Do you want to earn $100 real easy."

He looked at me funny, like it was a set up. "Seriously, my friend here," pointing to Annie who was showing off her huge boobs popping out of her dress, "her ex didn't pay his child support and he's behind 3 months. I just need you to see if he is inside and let us know. That's all. Here's his photo and here's $50 now an $50 when you come back with a yes or no answer. Neither of us is allowed in from a previous incident."

The picture I took from a picture frame I kept for just this purpose. He really needed the money so he grabbed the $50. I grabbed his other wrist injecting the EOL and said, "Please, this is really important. Take this photo. I'll wait 10 minutes if I don't get chased away."   His response was a head nod, he never spoke thinking I might be recording him.

As soon as he went inside, we left the area and straight back to the jet. The hotel room was for one night and I called them saying there was an emergency and we wouldn't be back and to close out my bill. I paid for the full night so that was cleared. I then called the detective and told him I was finished and he could return home thanking him for his excellent work.

Annie had a very small role in this job but it was an important one. It was more believable when Fenner saw her and was probably surprised by her boobs just staring back. He never took his eyes off them except to grab the $50 and glance at me.

Another job completed so we returned to the jet. Candy was on standby and she greeted us for the return flight. The flight back went very quickly while I worked on the file to close out the job. Andy was notified that Fenner will be dead in less than 24 hours from now. He anxiously awaits final proof.

Chapter 52

Annie and I finally had some time for ourselves. Date night tonight. Dinner and a movie sounded great with some drinks at Gordon Biersch in Market Commons. She drove over to my place in the afternoon and we laid out on the beach for about an hour. The weather was incredible. Bright sunshine, a soft breeze and the waves were docile.

She asked me to put some tanning lotion on her back and legs. It turned into a foreplay type of massage. She told me to slow down and let her have some sun. I let her be and took a dip in the ocean. The waves sucked but it felt great to be in the water. It seems so wrong I never get in the ocean enough and its right outside my back door.

Annie was ready to turn over and I offered to add lotion on the front but she said she got it. Maybe tonight I'll get to massage her front side later I'm thinking with a smiling grin on my face. We grabbed the towels and moved to the hot tub. We talked about her dad's condition and her mom doing the best she could.

Mom had told her for now she was OK but with him getting worse, she could need some help soon. I had already decided to tell Annie to send her mom a check offering support to make her life easier now. We had the money and spending it for a good reason made total sense. Annie listened intently to my proposal and started to fill up with tears.

This has been weighing on her more than I realized. The decision was done. We set up an account giving her mother full authority to use as she sees fit. $500,000 to start with and she just needed to let us know if more was needed. The whole question was about quality of life. Annie brought that point up and asked me if I would administer the EOL if it came to that.

I was taken by surprise of the suggestion at first and then explained it wasn't meant for any reason other than to complete a job I was assigned to. I told her that once I go down that path, the line of when to use EOL could start to become blurred. She understood and we changed the subject. She did feel relieved about getting the account for mom to use as needed.

We had a very intense moment discussing her parent's situation. It's never easy to handle the subject of Alzheimer's and quality of life decisions. I felt her pain and concerns.

She said, "Come join me for a shower." "I have a couple phone calls to make, start without me," "OK." I contacted my lawyer and had him start the process to set the account up for her mom. It took longer than I expected and I missed my shower time with her. Annie walked out in her robe and I was just hanging up the phone.

"Sorry honey, I had business to finish." "What kind of business?" "I just got off the phone with my lawyer making arrangements for your mom's account, "I said to her. She smiled and rushed over to plant a big kiss on my lips and said, "Thank you, thank you, thank you." We embraced and kissed some more as tears ran down her cheeks. She started to say I love you out loud and stopped. I did hear her say it in a whisper as she walked away.

Those three words have been unspoken for fear it would change our entire relationship. Maybe it's about time we say it to each other. I know I think about it more and more. For now it can wait. We still have our whole life ahead of us. When the time is right, Right?

I jumped in the shower before getting ready for our date. When I came out, Annie was staring me down from head to toe and back. I was still naked and drying off. She dropped her robe and came over to me pushing her luscious boobs into my chest. We connected our hands with our arms alongside of our hips, fingers interlaced and started kissing.

I moved our interlaced hands to her back and pulled her tight to my body. Then I said, "Are you ready for some fun?" "What do have in mind honey?" I laid her on the bed and said, "Close your eyes sweetie." She obeyed my command and I said, "Wait, I'll be back in a minute." She probably wondered what I doing. I returned back in less than a minute.

I found the remote control vibrator toy and put it in her with the final step of locking it in place. The key was put on the dresser. She remembered the sexual effect it had last time and was excited about a repeat performance. I remembered it too and have been dying to do it again. We got dressed in casual clothing. Too her casual also included a low cut dress tight fitting that hugged her ass.

For everyone else, she was eye candy, for me, she was my girl. It was rare for me to get jealous when other dudes gave her attention. It does happen on occasion and it puts a rush in me reminding me I'm alive. Deep down I trust her completely but still I have an element of jealously that keeps it real.

Time was lost in getting ready. Gordon Biersch was very busy so we sat at the bar waiting for a table. We decided to have dinner there. The food is very good and their menu has plenty of choices to pick from. We finished a bottle of Pinot Noir and the signal came our table was ready.

We both had the Flame Grilled New York Strip and another bottle of wine. Annie's birthday was less than a month away. I pulled out a brochure for a vacation to Italy. She asked, "What's this?" "I wanted to surprise you for your birthday," and her eyes lit up in anticipation. "With our crazy schedule, I wanted plan the perfect time together."

"This is awesome honey, when did you want to go?" "It's not about me baby, it's about you. Think about it and I'll book the reservations. "Ok, I will like wow, I'm stunned." "It's special seeing you happy like this." The waitress came to take our order. I was a little naughty when I turned on the remote on low. She forgot about it and it caused her to jump in her chair.

This was the new top of the line model and it had no humming sound for others to hear. Only the sensation from the vibration excited Annie and slowly built the passion. I turned on the wave and a rhythmic vibration was now in motion. She begged me to turn it off for now. I could have been a bastard and let it flow but I had plenty of time to play later.

Leaving the restaurant, we made a stop into Victoria Secrets. It seemed like everything was on sale with all the signs throughout the store. Annie had her favorite spots in the store to shop from and it didn't take long to find an outfit to model for me later tonight. Dinner and shopping was done. We finished 2 bottles of wine and Annie was definitely buzzed.

Annie wanted to see the girly movie, a comedy with Julia Roberts. I love a good love story too. Hey, I'm allowed. I really like it in a comedy. The theater was half full. We found our usual place in the top back corner seats. I turned the remote on low again. She was a little more prepared but still jumped at the first hint of a vibrating motion.

Then I took the level to the top and she could barely contain herself. She punched me in the arm and I just laughed. She tried reaching for the remote and I held it away from her. To the others nearby, it looked like she was attacking me. I turned it off for now. The anticipation of it getting turned back on at any moment was in her head the entire movie.

The movie over so we headed home. I turned the wave motion back on and she was ready this time. I raised the volume to about 40% for the trip home. It was about a 15 minute ride. I hoped she could contain herself from having an orgasm until we made it home. She pulled my shorts down before lowering her head started moving in rhythm with her vibrator.

Now I was worried I couldn't make it home. A police cruiser pulled up alongside us at the red light. I could barely contain myself and kept a straight face telling Annie to stay down, a cop was next to us. She was laughing hysterically. That actually got a further rise from me.

The light turned green and I let him pull ahead of me and turned onto Ocean Boulevard to get out of his view. Now I just had all the people walking on the boulevard to avoid being seen. I'm sure they would get a kick out of it. Reaching the house, we both hurried into the house.

She handed me the lotion for a massage. I wasted no time in pouring the lotion and massaging her body. I turned the vibrator to max and continued massaging. I was fully erect and tried to have patience before we made love. The foreplay is always worth it. When I put my hand down between her legs, I felt the vibrator and then noticed how intense it was for Annie.

I played with her some more. She absolutely loved it. It was time to remove the device and I grabbed the key to unlock it, removing it from her. I was ready to have my turn after all the foreplay. It felt so good.

It was a magical night and we slept great. My dreams that night were of Annie and I as husband and wife in a beach house with our bed overlooking the ocean in some Caribbean location where the neighbors are an acre away from us. Never stop dreaming.

Chapter 53

The next morning I checked my messages and then the news. The story about Fenner was on HLN and they were debating his release from the penitentiary. It was national news headlines. The release of a rapist back into his same environment was a recipe for disaster.

The story goes on to say he died from a heart attack (autopsy pending), while attempting to rape a 14 year old girl he coerced into joining him for some drugs. The girl was no angel but rape is just wrong on every count. He had gotten as far as ripping off her top and was sitting on her knees when the EOL timer kicked in and he had the heart attack. He fell on top of her and freaking her out even more.

She stood no chance if that didn't happen. When the police arrived on the scene, they could hear her crying hysterically and pulled him off her. The girl's face had been punched causing her to black out at one point and woke back up with him ripping off clothing. She was lucky but she'll always be a victim from the memory of what had happened.

Annie peered over my shoulder to see the storyline unfold. She felt for the poor girl and realized that our efforts saved her just in time. She hugged me from behind and said, "Thanks for being you." Being a paid executioner is sometimes hard to get a grip on. Knowing I ended someone's life puts conflict in my life. I try to justify it every way I can. It's not an easy thing to do.

When I see the end of the story from the jobs I have done and particularly as in the rape case, I find solace in knowing I helped save other people from bad things happening to them. It's a lot like going to war. People die trying to do what they think is doing the right thing and killing the enemy. The believable cause wins out over the end of someone's life.

Tonight I had a group of college kids with a 21st birthday party and an engagement celebration as a reason to party into the night in Broadway at the Beach. The pickup time was scheduled for 11:30 just before midnight of her 21st. I called to confirm and they were all excited.

We received confirmation our account received the funds and Andy, our client, was most appreciative. I also talked with my lawyer and the account for Annie's mom and dad was officially set. Funds were now available to her. I let Annie know the good news and she called her mom. She was blown away at the amount and couldn't stop being thankful.

I told Annie to visit her mom and help her with ideas to give her dad the best quality of life possible with his dwindling health. The jet is at your disposal whenever you want. She immediately started planning a trip for about 3 days for now. I reminded her about setting a date for her birthday trip to Italy.

All seemed right in the world. Another bad person could no longer hurt anyone ever again, our assets grew again, Annie and I had a chart topping night last night and we were able to help her mom and dad.

My group was ready at Destiny Lane for a great night. A group photo for facebook and my website was being staged in front of the Limo. An additional few house parties nearby brought another 25 to 30 people for the photo. I was even in the center of the group when the multitude of photos was taken. It made for great PR on my website.

My group shuffled in and the music was cranked up. Local police were posted nearby looking for any trouble and underage drinking. They don't play games if you're under 21 around here. I bumped fist with the dude turning 21 and got a hug from the engaged couple. They met me as juniors and are graduating this year. I wished them the best.

The trip to Broadway at the Beach was like a group karaoke event. The music was so load, it drowned out all the bad singers and the ones who forgot some of the words, The partying started hours ago and a few were questionable if they could get into the clubs. If they appear too intoxicated, they could be refused.

The girls were dressed to impress. They wore short skirts, high heels, gorgeous hair and the guys, jeans and shorts. Some of the guys wore dumb ass t-shirts and other collared shirts. I swear the dresses get shorter every year. I'll see them all in a few hours.

Broadway, in particular the last two clubs still open, Malibu's and Rodeo, had last call at 2:30. By 3 the tables needed to be cleared of all remaining alcohol. The final surge of clubbers came out at 3 and my group was among them. We lost a couple who hooked up with someone else and replaced them with other friends needing a ride back to Destiny La.

It was a more typical ride home. Some passed out. Some were in a drama mode for boyfriend and girlfriend arguments caused by jealousy and alcohol. Some were watching others I pointed out to make sure they don't spew in the Limo. Most of the rest were busy texting to God know who at 3:30 in the morning. Thanks, high 5's and hugs symbolized our farewell.

Chapter 54

I received a text about 4:30 a.m. My initial thought was it was Annie or The Grinch. It also could have been from my group who may have lost a phone or camera. It was from Molly. Call me. 911, it's an emergency. She was crying hysterically when she answered the phone. She was trying to tell me something but the crying made it impossible to understand.

"Annie, Annie was hit, car, hospital," is all I could make out. "Molly, take a deep breath and slow down. What happened?" "She was hit by a drunk driver and they rushed her to the hospital by helicopter." My heart sunk. This couldn't be real. Not my Annie, Not my Love. Molly said, "She's knocked out." "I'm on the way to the hospital now," is the last thing I could say.

I was there in half the time. My heart was beating so fast. My emotions were scared, lost, worried, freaking out but trying to be calm and dozens more, all of them were racing through my mind and body. I can't lose her, I hope she is going to be ok. I LOVE HER SO MUCH!

Inside the hospital, they wouldn't let me see her. I wasn't family in the laws eyes plus they were running tests, lots of tests. She still hasn't regained consciousness and the doctors were worried about hemorrhaging in the brain from impact against the door window.

Hours passed and the doctors finally came out and told us she was in intensive care. The next 8 hours are important to see how she reacts to the medications. She was still not conscious and they took care of her broken arm and leg. We asked if she was going to be alright. The doctor responded, "It's just too early to tell. Physically yes, mentally we don't know just yet."

He used too many long medical terms which left Molly, Bridgette and I even more concerned. She was T-boned by some asshole drunk. "When I could see her?" I frantically asked. They asked who I was and told them I was her fiancé and her mom and dad were in California. I am paying for all doctors bills and signed all the appropriate paperwork.

That made sure I got around the no family yet rule. A nurse led me to her room. I was allowed to sit alongside the bed and hold her hand. I kissed her on her forehead and touched her lips full of hoses attached to the hospital equipment. Monitors were everywhere and nurses and doctors zooming back and forth. They kept checking in on her looking for any signs of consciousness.

So much was going on in my mind. I never told her I loved her and that tore me up. Will I get the chance to tell her? Will I get to marry her some day? Will we have children together? Will my friend smile again? How do I tell her mom what happened? Question after question controlled my brain. She has to get better, she just has to.

I held her hand and whispered, "I love you Annie. I need you Annie. Please get better Annie." I couldn't stop repeating those words. I wanted her to know I was here. Somehow I would make it all right. Please DON'T GIVE UP. I'm not going anywhere babe. I tweeted for everyone to pray for Annie. To see her bandage on her head was killing me.

The nurses would have me step out from time to time to do their thing. The lobby was full of her friends and seeing their concerned faces hit me even harder. It was great seeing everyone who cared about Annie. She was always there for all of us in times of despair. Now it was our turn to be there for her and prayers.

She made it through the first hurdle of 8 hours. No change and they said that was actually a good thing. I need my baby to come alive again. My baby was going to be just fine. The doctors said she is now has a 50/50 chance of being fine. The next hurdle is 48 hours minus the 8 already passed. There was hope. That was all we had was hope.

I contacted The Grinch and my boss at the Limo Company and said I am taking a leave of absence until she is healthy again no matter how long it takes. Everyone understood and offered help in any way. The thought came into my mind of the drunken idiot who smashed into her. I was ready to track him down and inject him with EOL.

If anyone deserved it, it was him. He was locked down in another room from his injuries awaiting a transport to jail. I slipped out to try and find him. I wanted to see who this idiot was. All I knew is he was a local in his early 20's. I found the room but the police wouldn't let me get near him. I felt the rage growing inside me. I needed to get away before I made a mistake.

I hurried back to my Annie. "I love you babe, I need you, I want you so much," I kept whispering to her. Hoping and praying for a sign of movement. Nothing. No response at all. I know she could hear me. I just know it and feel it. She needs to know how I feel. How bad I want to hold her and kiss those precious lips with a deep passionate kiss.

It's been 30 hours. Emotionally I was drained. I was determined to will her to health. I started remembering our days on the beach, our moment in the hot tub, the time with her parents, the incredible sex and dozens of scenes with her smile in it. It's not fair to love someone so much and have this happen. Where is the justice in that?

I was lost in my thoughts when all of a sudden an alarm went off. Doctors and nurses scrambled around the bed unhooking some machines and rolled her out with complete urgency.   "What happened? Please tell me!" They stopped me from following Annie being wheeled out. "Sir, let us do our job. Wait in the lobby. We'll let you know as soon as we can."

All I heard was, "Dr. Ames to the OR stat!" over the hospital speakers. "Is it bad? Can you save her? What's wrong? Where are you taking her? Somebody! Anybody!" My efforts were in vain. Not one would answer. Is this the last time I'd see my Annie alive? Falling to my knees, I broke down into tears looking up to the heavens for an answer.

"I LOVE YOU ANNIE!"

Final Thoughts

I end this story on an upsetting note. My poor Annie is in surgery and I can do nothing to help her. All the money in the world offers no guarantee she'll live and be her normal self. I love this woman for better or worse. She is my best friend, partner and lover.

Molly and Bridgette are hurting for their best friend.

The Grinch still has a business to run and bad people keep him busy. Maybe I'll get to meet him someday. He'll have to be without my services for a while.

Life in Myrtle Beach will go on and the zany partying will continue to happen. More drunken fools will be enjoying their vacation freedoms. More stories will be told and remembered as the fun times never end.

Please pray for Annie to survive her tragedy. I hope you enjoyed the many insane stories. You can check for updates at Limostories.com. As soon as we know the condition of Annie, we'll update the website. Please tell others about our stories so we can gather support for new stories to be lived and told in the future.

Remember –

"What happens in Myrtle Beach, stays in Myrtle Beach, or does it?"

And please don't forget, this is fiction!

Made in the USA
Columbia, SC
26 December 2018